MW01505482

ALSO BY KENAN ORHAN

I Am My Country and Other Stories

THE RENOVATION

THE
RENOVATION

A NOVEL

KENAN ORHAN

Farrar, Straus and Giroux
New York

Farrar, Straus and Giroux
120 Broadway, New York 10271

EU Representative: Macmillan Publishers Ireland Ltd, 1st Floor, The Liffey
Trust Centre, 117–126 Sheriff Street Upper, Dublin 1, D01 YC43

Library of Congress Cataloging-in-Publication Data
Names: Orhan, Kenan, 1993– author
Title: The renovation : a novel / Kenan Orhan.
Description: First edition. | New York : Farrar, Straus and Giroux, 2026.
Identifiers: LCCN 2025038092 | ISBN 9780374609429 hardcover
Subjects: LCGFT: Novels | Fiction | Surrealist literature
Classification: LCC PS3615.R494 R46 2026
LC record available at https://lccn.loc.gov/2025038092

Designed by Patrice Sheridan

Our books may be purchased in bulk for specialty retail/wholesale, literacy,
corporate/premium, educational, and subscription box use. Please contact
MacmillanSpecialMarkets@macmillan.com.

www.fsgbooks.com
Follow us on social media at @fsgbooks

10 9 8 7 6 5 4 3 2 1

This is a work of fiction. All of the names, characters, organizations,
places, and events portrayed in this work are either products of the
author's imagination or used fictitiously.

THIS BOOK IS DEDICATED
TO CAREGIVERS

PART I

I DON'T KNOW BY what accident the builders had managed it, but instead of a remodeled bathroom attached to my bedroom, they had installed a prison cell. They had told me it would take a month (thank goodness we had a second bathroom, though we did find ourselves exploiting the kindness of a neighboring flat every now and again when one of us was taking a particularly long shower), and I had pestered them the whole time; my offers of tea or snacks were obvious ploys to steal peeks at their work. But they had almost superstitiously prevented me from checking on their progress, even hanging a tarp over the bathroom door to make a sort of antechamber, so that no glimpse of the room within was possible. It was for the dust, they said. "Like an air lock." I tried to sneak in when they left for the day; however, they had installed a new lock on the door to which only they had the key. I knew it was just as much for their own benefit. I didn't blame them; who could work well under constant scrutiny? I tried to respect their privacy, they were working through the Christmas season after all, and no doubt unhappy about it, but it did make me anxious for some hint of progress, any sliver of an update they could give me, compounded by the fact that we really couldn't afford this renovation and had had to make a number of financial adjustments to accommodate it.

The hysterical sounds of tile saws and the rhythmic grunting and thudding of people moving heavy things continued right up to the very last moment, as if a bathroom remodel has absolutely no delicate parts, is just force after force after force, until finally, at the end of the fifth week, I could hear the slapdash sounds of tools clattering into their boxes and bags, a shushing bit of broom-work, and then all the laborers appeared out from under the tarp in a jittery huddle and said it was done, the final bill could be expected in two weeks, and they dashed off to their next job as if they were Supermans and some poor awaiting kitchen was a plane falling out of the sky.

With high expectations, I dragged the tarp aside, threw open the door, and burst into the room. Where my shower and double vanity should have been, instead there was the perfect tableau of a prison cell. It was about four meters wide and four meters long with a bed on a metal frame along one side. A shiny metal apparatus that was both toilet and sink wrapped into one was separated from the bed by a narrow partition. Opposite were a little table and swing-out seat, both anchored to the wall. It was modeled after Silivri Prison in Istanbul. There was no mistaking it (try as I might to rub this image out of my eyes).

I stood there motionless for a moment, then turned and walked back out. I closed the door and replaced the tarp over it. It was late afternoon and my husband would be home from work soon. He might be a bit oblivious, wrapped up as he is in a spool of his nerves, but my husband had been just as curious about the progress of the renovation as I was, if not more so, going so far as to watch a series of lock-picking videos on YouTube to see if he could get past the contractor's lock (though he did not end up buying the hooks, rakes, or tension tools). As soon as he knew they were finished, he would want to inspect the bathroom (that he had a hand in designing), perhaps open a bottle of prosecco. I lifted the tarp once more, cracked the door open, and surveyed the bungled renovation. I was angry more than anything, angry at how inconsiderate people could be, angry at the malicious oversight that had caused this calamity.

I don't think of myself as a particularly reticent person—indeed, I often find myself too forthcoming with my opinions—but I knew at once I had to hide this from my husband. Don't get me wrong, he's a very understanding man, sometimes too understanding, and though he would understand this—whatever that meant—he has a nervous disposition that manifests as bouts of hypochondria. This was precisely the sort of thing to trigger his anxiety so that his stomach is nothing but ulcers and acids in flux, and on his tongue would be the refrain: "Dear me! Dear me! O, deary, deary me!"

I called the builder, but it rang without end. Then I called one of the plumbers, and one of the carpenters, and the tile guy, and anyone else whose number I had, but every call went to voicemail.

This couldn't have been happening at a worse time. We had decided to renovate the bathroom (even though we couldn't afford it) because my father could no longer live on his own. He'd insisted he wasn't some invalid who needed to be doted on or else sealed up in a dank little hospice room, so when the three of us arrived in Baronissi in 2017, he'd bought his own flat across the village from ours, in a former monastery, but he was, even then, already quite dependent on us.

I had been unable to find work in the village. Admittedly, I was holding out hope to remain in my field. I had been a school psychologist back in Turkey, and had occasionally contracted out to hospitals to do specialized testing for kids in the psychiatric ER, but with my limited Italian, the different tests and licenses between the countries, and the dearth of children in the village compared to Istanbul, it soon became clear it was foolish for me to keep trying. My husband had been an accountant in Istanbul, though he grew up in his father's garage in Ankara. I have a picture of him as a boy on my nightstand, covered in grease with shining engine parts sticking out of his pockets. When we settled in Italy, he immediately took a job with a local mechanic while I stayed home hunting for Turkish-language positions, which is to say I deluded myself. So it didn't feel wholly uncaring or irresponsible to allow my father to get his own place and practice a little independence. I was always available; I could check on him and bring him food or go and collect him and plop him in front of my television while I mopped the floors and did the laundry and aired out the rooms, much as I might have done with a child for a playdate.

But in the months leading up to the renovation, I had been collecting him with greater frequency, making more of his meals each week, and having him stay the night a few times each month. In reality, this was the first step of his moving in with us. Over the last ten years, my father's faculties had been ebbing away. It was painstaking, but not gradual, not in the sense of something steadily, as a ramp or graph, easing downward. Some days he was himself or more so, back to that darting intelligence of his youth, walking down the stairs and up the street to the bakery without much of a fuss, though he needed his cane still, but most importantly, on the good days, he could do this without forgetting where he was going or how to return. Other days he was replaced by this husk, a father-shaped mannequin or a crash test dummy, always tipping over and falling on the hard floor of the kitchen, or against the rim of the bathtub, or into tables laid with white lace doilies and brittle vessels balanced atop them, as brittle as the bones of an old man. Other days still there was nothing exceptional about his physical health, but sitting in his chair he would stare for extended periods without moving or blinking, and I could see something begin to churn beneath his face. I could see a man who had lost a word. Then another and another and another. Even before we left Istanbul, my father spoke fewer than half the sentences he used to, couldn't remember such easy words as *onion*, *house key*, *bedsheet*. He became very quiet, a stark contrast to the expressive and passionate man I had grown up with. He seemed to be retreating into himself, as if his body were a ship taking on water and, in order not to drown, had begun sealing up the flooding compartments and so abandoning them to seawater.

One night last autumn, having canceled plans for lunch with him and then forgotten to stop by before dinner, I realized very late that I had not yet checked on my father. I hurried over to his apartment a few streets away. When I knocked, he didn't shout from inside or come to the door. I didn't wait long, but something about the moment felt protracted and distant, as if I were very far away from myself, though I don't much believe in premonition. Maybe it was the change in our routine that made me suspicious. I fumbled with the keys as I let myself in. All the lights were out. The flat was submerged in a wet darkness. Through the glistening shadows, I could see him lying on his back, one of his arms limply stuck into the air, paddling as if he were trying to swim. He looked metallic almost, dimly shining. He was covered in blood. This sharp regret large as a railroad spike pierced me, releasing all the air from my body. I could feel the suffocation curling my fingers, climbing up the long cords of muscles in my arms, bending my whole body over.

We were fortunate. He'd broken his nose and it bled profusely, but in the darkness everything looked much worse than it was. The ER nurses said, broken nose aside, he looked fine. They said that standing between me and him. The lights of the hospital room were so blinding that everything looked two-dimensional, impossible to pick up and hold. My father's eyes were bloodshot, his face purple and swollen, fresh stitching creeping over the rim of his lip, and two wads of gauze stuffed into his still-bleeding nose. He looked like a ghoul. They said everything that was already wrong with him was still wrong with him but nothing new was wrong with him and he could go home.

He moved in with us, transforming the dining room into his hospice with his electronic bed and chair. The main bathroom quickly filled up with his pills and slip-prevention devices and other medical clutter, and so we decided to expand our en suite (architecturally little more than a toilet crammed into a broom closet) into a second bathroom just for us. All the while we kept saying to each other that he might get better as a way of convincing ourselves of its truth, but his condition was by now very poor. Eight years of Alzheimer's didn't leave much else to be expected. The doctors didn't say that. *It's not so bad right now*—that's what the doctors said, knowing it would get worse—but they didn't ask my father or me, and that's not what either of us would have said: *It's not so bad right now.*

Trying to remain calm, I decided that maybe the builders were playing a joke. They had learned about my husband's research into lock picking, and knew I listened at the jamb while they worked, and they were pulling one of those pranks you see on social media that has everyone in the comments laughing even though it is in fact a complete destruction of the victims' lives.

"Alright, you can come out now!" I shouted, and threw the bathroom door wide open. No grinning builders emerged from a secret compartment. I shouted again, "Very funny, out you come!" After a minute, I stepped into the room ensconced in all the trappings of a prison cell with even a guard walking by the bars just then. Relief flooded through me.

"Aha, you got me!" My voice carried far away, faintly echoing in the uncarpeted room.

The guard, who really could have been my contractor in disguise, seemed genuinely shocked to see me. "What, what is this?" he exclaimed in Turkish. He paused with a stupefied look on his face, and I asked him in Italian to explain himself. Confused, he asked me in Turkish what I wanted.

"Where am I?" I responded in Turkish.

"Are you sick? Silivri Prison."

I was growing impatient. "That's not right. This is supposed to be a waterfall shower with two heads and massaging jets and a marble bench."

"Massaging jets, ha ha! No, this is the prison."

"But what's it doing in my bathroom?" I asked.

"It isn't," he said. I pointed behind me at the doorway I had just walked through and my bedroom beyond it. He looked into the cell and frowned. "Now, how did they mess up like that?"

"The builders just finished today. The plumber turned on the water a moment ago," I said.

"Well, how do you know your bathroom isn't in Silivri Prison instead of the other way round?"

It was a natural enough question that nevertheless irritated me. Couldn't the oaf see that there were far greater consequences on my side of the bars? I mean, I was the one now without a bathroom while his fictitious prison still had plenty of cells. "Put yourself in my place," I said.

"Oh ho, yes, that's a good one! As if a guard has never heard a prisoner say that. You'll have to be cleverer than that to get out of here."

At that I lost my temper, rushed forward, and threw myself against the cell bars, nearly throttling myself, but they wouldn't budge. Up close, I could see the guard was standing in a corridor that extended beyond my field of vision on either side. It was hard to understand how they had fit all this into our tiny en suite.

"Keep this to yourself," he said, as if talking about an elephant behind window curtains. "I don't need the headache of explaining this to the warden. I have enough problems as it is without you stirring up trouble."

As soon as he said "trouble," I ran out of the cell, back into my bedroom, slammed the door shut, and pulled the plastic tarp down. My husband would be home from work in maybe ten minutes. Too long to make a snap decision, and not long enough to rationalize a plan. I went to the main bathroom, where my father stood staring in the mirror. I said *Hello, how are you, do you need anything, a blanket, tea, a bit of a sandwich?* as I took out the P trap under his sink, then went to the kitchen and grabbed our toolbox, and in a mad dash (really my husband was late at this point and would be home any second) I threw a bunch of ratchets and nuts and bolts and screwdrivers and pliers and the P trap next to the tarp in our bedroom to make it look like the plumbing would need a few more days to finish. Moments later, I heard my husband open the front door, and I flew down the hall to him and planted a kiss on his cheek. He gave my chin a pet, and I took his briefcase from him (he liked having a briefcase though he had absolutely no use for the thing). I told him the plumber had made a mistake and that we would have to keep using my father's bathroom.

He sighed and asked me about my day and then we settled into our happy, if well-worn habits, but obviously the only thing on my mind was the prison. Each sound in the flat made the surface of my skin fizzle. A real, live prison guard was looming just beyond my door. Did that mean there would be a prisoner moving into our bathroom? The walls of the flat were not soundproof; would we hear them whispering to themselves? What if a guard started hollering in the corridor or, worse, sounded an alarm? What if a fight should break out? There was no way I could convince my husband these were merely the sounds of a defective toilet. Worse, what if someone on the other side heard us in our flat, and sent the guards pouring through into our bedroom like cops in a Buster Keaton movie? Fortunately, however, my prison was a quiet one, or by some other miracle the sound did not carry through the door, and we got through the night without incident.

———

The next morning was a gruelingly slow pantomime of our routines. I wanted my husband out, out the door and off to work right away, but he always paused between his coffee and his breakfast to read a little bit of a magazine (literary in some way) or a page or two in a very long book with which he seemed never to make any headway. The whole time I pretended to be decluttering my wardrobe, making decisions about which items I might be able to consign to a used-goods shop and which I could repair and which I could dress up with a few new accessories, narrating everything aloud so that my husband might be very bored and would stay out of our bedroom. I was absolutely sure that some loud noise would burst out from the en suite at any moment: a morning alarm or loudspeaker to wake the prisoners or perhaps a call to prayer (I hadn't thought about that once in my life till now; did they have muezzins in prison?).

My father emerged from his room and trundled toward the kitchen. "Coffee!" he yelled to me, as if I were a lazybones sleeping in. My husband had only made a single cup for himself. He was an enormously self-sufficient man and rarely noticed when he might be useful to others.

"Yes, this blouse would do well with a little vest, I think!" I shouted back, pacing back and forth in our bedroom and slamming the door closed with an "oops!" then stuffing more comments under the gap at the floor: "I must get a new pair of flats, or better an old pair that is new to me!"

"Coffee!" my father shouted again.

My husband, having at last finished reading one page

(today it was the long book), packed his toast and jam into his mouth, grabbed his briefcase, in which he kept his book and a magazine and a crossword he never finished, and left for work, shouting at me: "Your dad wants coffee!"

Pacing outside my renovated bathroom, I gave it a couple of minutes to be sure he wasn't coming back. Then I called my contractor, then tried every member of the crew whose numbers I could track down, before resorting to calling my contractor over and over until at last he answered with a casual hello as if he had no knowledge of what he'd done to my home.

"You've bungled my renovation!" I started.

"I don't think so," he said. Fair enough; he didn't know who I was. I told him my name and address and repeated that he had ruined my bathroom.

He said he recognized my voice.

A brittle crash came from the kitchen. My father was undoubtedly trying to make himself coffee. Ignoring the sound, I demanded my contractor justify this egregious mistake. Another, smaller crunch like a wristwatch being crushed in the kitchen, and I could hear my father mumbling between sharp gasps. I asked the contractor to repeat himself as I went to check on my father. He was standing under the kitchen window, taking great care to bend as he reached into the little dishwasher, emptying it though it had not run, and putting soiled plates and pans into our neat little cabinets. He doubled over to grab a large bowl but struggled and couldn't straighten back up. His cane, the sort that has a few wide feet so that it can stand on its own, was abandoned yet again at the other

14

end of the kitchen—blocking the path between the cabinets and the wall. I brought it back to him and took the bowl out of his hands and put it in the sink. Unoffended, he carefully lifted the bowl back out of the sink and put it in the high cupboard where it did not belong.

"They're not clean," I whispered in the threatening hushed voice that respectable adults use on not-so-respectable children in public. I apologized to the contractor and said my service was cutting out, but as he started re-explaining himself, my father fired up the coffee grinder. I could hardly hear the other end of the line, and now my father returned to clattering the porcelain and silverware in the dishwasher. Speeding back to my room, I ducked beneath the tarp and into the prison cell, where all was finally quiet. As mystifying as it was to find a prison now installed in my bathroom, I was more surprised that they had managed to sneak it out of Turkey in the first place. My contractor was telling me that he always verified everything with the customer, that he required receipts with signatures to that effect, and that he had just emailed me scans of my signature, indicating I had approved the installed materials and fixtures.

"Yes, materials and fixtures perhaps, but they put them to use all wrong! They've made some horrible parody of my design. I wanted a bidet, not a prison washbasin. It is a jail cell!"

"That is a rude exaggeration, though I can barely understand it with your accent."

"No," I insisted. "There is an actual prison where there should be a bathroom. It even has a guard!"

"That seems highly unlikely to have happened in any case," said the contractor, and he rang off.

Then, as if the notion of coffee (spurred by the grinder) had popped out of my head and begun wandering the house on its own, a small cup of Turkish coffee appeared in the corner of the cell. It was a beautiful cup with blue arabesques on a neat little saucer with a matching pattern. Where had it come from? The guard must have brought it for me, but I hadn't seen him come by, nor had I heard the soft scrape of porcelain being set down on concrete, nor, as I thought about it, did it make sense that coffee service was a staple of Turkish prisons. The coffee was simply there and the guard was not. I took a sip and felt awash in giddiness. It was the precise duplicate of the coffee served at Mandabatmaz, in Beyoğlu, with its thick foam the consistency of a luxurious dream. It was a favorite café in my family, though it had only four chairs and served nothing but coffee. For a moment it really was like being back there, and all at once I felt the enormous distances of time and space between myself and Istanbul, and felt these distances collapsed if only briefly. I took the coffee inside to my father. I made him hold it, and I mimed drinking.

"Isn't it just like at Mandabatmaz?" I asked.

He took a sip and made a face. "It isn't correct," he said. This was a phrase he had come to rely on as much as he did his cane. His thoughts had become slippery as eels in silvery rivers and the words to wrangle them had wriggled out of his head, leaving precious few phrases that now had to stand in for so much more, for all the sputtering thoughts that he could no longer articulate.

"Isn't it just how they used to make it?" I asked again, trying to coax something out of him, hoping to jolt his memory. Mandabatmaz had been one of my father's regular haunts, the first café I remember him taking me to, the only café, really, that made its coffee any differently than all the others. Gently I asked, did he remember our favorite café in Beyoğlu, the taste of their coffee?

He looked at me, knowingly at first. He lifted the cup to his lips again and his face changed. His disappointment was obvious. He raised his eyebrows and pouted his lips and said nothing. He kept repeating these small gestures of the face, pulling his wits about him into a tidy little pile, trying to make something of them, but he only managed to raise his eyebrows and pout his lips and say nothing.

I took the cup from him, ready to finish it myself, but inexplicably it was empty: not just the coffee but the grounds too.

The first time we took my father to the hospital was almost a decade ago. In 2013 we were still in our flat in Istanbul, on a curved street over a tree-choked cemetery. It had originally been his flat, and his father's before that, as was almost everything in his life (his neckties were all as old as him or even older). My mother died in 2003, and about six months later he'd mentioned selling the flat and moving the two of us into a house up the coast toward the Black Sea. I'd begged him to wait, wait until I was done with high school and off to university. Every few years after that, he'd say again he was thinking of selling the flat, and

I'd eventually convince him to wait, but after I finished my graduate psychology program, married my husband, and moved in with him, my father said he really couldn't stand it anymore. His parents had died in the flat, his wife after them. "I am outnumbered by the dead and this is bad for my liver. Too many memories in this home—even at the corners and all up the baseboards they are piling." With a bit of the savings he'd squirreled away, he bought himself a small place in a retirement community in Üsküdar across the Bosporus from us: "It is a necessary change of scenery," he said.

My father moved out, and my husband and I left our tiny closet near Dolmabahçe and took over the flat I had grown up in (no rent and thrice the space). When my father called, we would ask how Asia was treating him, and he would ask us if Europe was still the Europe it ever was. We visited him for dinner now and again, bringing things that would reheat well, trying to supplement our separation from him and make the time between our visits feel shorter. Eventually geography dictated our relationship. My father and I talked less frequently, went on fewer outings together. "I'm a ferry ride away," he said as some effort at consolation or accusation—it was difficult to tell which.

"As am I," I replied, upset at his suggestion. In fact, he took the ferry over every morning on his way to work at the university. He had the time and ability to commute for classes, but not to see his daughter. He didn't even stop by on his way home, though the university was a quick cab ride from our flat. I had been suggesting he do just that for weeks, but of course it was not an option for him. He moved out to get away from ghosts, and it was insensitive of me to forget that. Yet when he learned that I had turned the second bedroom into a workout studio he was outraged.

"And where am I supposed to sleep when I visit?"

"You don't visit."

But I didn't visit him either. I was too busy at work, rushing between schools and hospitals, and I knew my aunts and uncle never went out to Üsküdar for tea or dinner. He had become a bit of a grouch—a fate I think he was prevented from realizing earlier in life by marrying my mother. As he was a political academic, it was easy to find his company stifling. The man always wanted serious and meaningful conversations, wanted to incite you to serious and meaningful change. If you didn't take a stake in your country, you didn't deserve much respect from it, a motto he invoked in response to everything from the price of gas to the new children's TV programs.

Distracted and negligent, I failed to call him for over three months, until eventually he called me and told me I was being rude. I remembered the comment about the ferry ride. Insensitive or obstinate as children can be toward their injured parents, I reminded him that phones worked in both directions, and he could've called me sooner than this.

"It is difficult," he said apologetically. "Something about dialing the house number . . . I worry your mother might pick up. Time . . . I mean . . . I am lost in time. I worry—if I dial—your mother might answer."

I made a concentrated effort to reach out to him after this, a drive to maintain our relationship, but my renewed and largely one-sided efforts finally dissipated and we did not speak to each other for a whole year, did not see each other for even longer, though we were distanced only by a cab over the bridge, or an undulating ferry across the wide and resplendent strait.

This changed when the protests started. It was a feral summer (as if the season itself is not always prone to bouts of wildness and ecstasy), and the city was inundated with people objecting to the way things were. My father, no doubt feeling lonely, no doubt feeling restless in sympathy with the restless city, had begun calling me and telling me to turn on the news. We would watch for an hour or so together. I didn't say much as the throng of people filled the square and pulsed like a giant ventricle, but my father talked the whole time, seemingly unbothered by my unenthusiastic *huh*s and *whoa*s, asking if I knew what was going on in my own neighborhood, if I knew what was changing in my city, if I knew how much the country had been eroded in these years under Erdoğan. I shrugged my shoulders even though he couldn't see it. I didn't really know what all this was about. I wanted to tell him it was easy for an old man to be politically aware; he didn't have anything better to do all day, he didn't have errands to run, dinner to cook, or a spouse who wanted to watch sitcoms instead of the news, but I couldn't say this. I knew he had only called in the first place because he missed my mother, the sole person in the family who would indulge him in his tirades, the sole person who kept up on every bit of news alongside him. I started inviting him over then. His loneliness was unhealthy, I thought. Plus, this way I could make sure he was eating well, not those frozen dinners he'd given himself over to in recent months. Somewhat to my surprise, he accepted these invitations. Side by side on the sofa, we watched the protests develop. While we could, we watched the mass of people grow and grow around Gezi Park. What had started as a few dozen environmentalists protecting a bit of grass and a few trees had, in less than a week, become over a hundred thousand people organizing in Istanbul each day with almost a million others joining them in cities like Izmir, Hatay, Bursa, Adana, and Antalya.

We opened up our laptops and phones and watched there as well—all the different news stations on simultaneously, everything at maximum volume. We saw everyone everywhere had dust masks or scarves or shirts tied over their mouths and noses and around their heads. They chanted, they sang, they clapped in unison like football fans. Park benches, street signs, pushcarts, ripped-up flagstones, garbage bins, car tires, and (ironically) tree branches were used as barricades at the entrances to Taksim Square or set on fire. Roving around in clumps, people hammered their fists against the gates of closed storefronts or on thin sheets of metal they'd brought from home. Others halted traffic in the streets encircling the square or incited the passing cars to honk, which they did. People played drums and guitars and flutes and horns. They played loud music and drank beer after beer from their backpacks. Many held up handwritten signs, little signs with jokes: "You banned alcohol, so people sobered up"; "We take that gas in a single hit, bro"; "Don't be scared, it's us! The People!" Thousands of phones constantly rang with alerts from Twitter and Facebook. Journalists shouted into microphones as swarms of people with TV cameras captured the boil. Groups danced as if in victory; others bickered bitterly. Everyone had a slogan or a mantra or a platitude. My father told me they were on guard for the future. He said this was the creation of a country—no! this *was* a country; a country is a constant struggle. And the people kept coming, pouring into the square from every avenue and alley that crisscrossed the neighborhood. A massive arrival of the city cramming into the park, and piling over the small walls, and jamming up the streets leading away, and spilling down into the gutters, and climbing atop cars and balconies and roofs, hanging from eaves and streetlamps, falling from the sky. Oh, was it loud, oh god was it a clamor without bounds that filled the whole city so that even if we tried to ignore it, even if we wanted to shrink down and hide away, there would be no escape from the noise. There was all day, every day, the roar of turmoil, and at the center of it stood the square and its people casting impossibly long shadows, as if the protest had made them into giants, a booming magnificence of red sheets, white crescents and stars.

Behind all this noise, however, in the shaded crevices of alleyways and on deserted side streets, policemen stood in knots, some waiting in blue uniforms and some in black body armor with white helmets and shields, some waiting with truncheons and some with rifles. Their liquid movements were out of a dream. Thin residues of tear gas clouds blew across the square. Behind this, the handful of gray police tanks with water cannons atop their turrets waited in the white sun.

When the TV channels we'd been following went out, we watched videos on news websites. When those were censored, we watched clips on Twitter until at last even that was shut down by government agencies. My husband was at his wits' end and spent the whole summer huddled in the bathtub in case of bombings (he had grown up in a certain era, in a certain household, where the state was the most fearful thing). I was impressed, I suppose, that so many people had gotten together without hurting one another. I was impressed that they had lasted so long in their barricades and camps, had repulsed or ignored a handful of halfhearted attempts by police to clear them out, but I could not find any desire to join them. I tried to stir up a bit of something like courage to go to the park—I knew it was what my father wanted to do, though he was too old— but I couldn't find this ounce of inspiration in me.

For his part, my father obsessed over following each development, learning the demands of the fractious groups— the anarchists, the communists, the environmentalists, the Kemalists, the Turanists, the socialists, the labor unions. He'd talk me through them, and I became the same confused child he'd tried to teach trigonometry, glazing over entirely as the words blurred into a nonsensical jumble, but occasionally he would confuse himself too, stumbling on all those names and acronyms, and if I noticed (which was rare) I would ask him if he'd had enough sleep lately, if he'd been eating—my father was not in the habit of taking care of himself; he had never had to do it while my mother was alive and had not picked it up after her death.

Sometimes he would forget something much simpler, like the name of a political party, as if the grain of sand on which this information was written had fallen out of his ear. There were so many factions, so many demands—politics in Turkey being nothing but a maze to me anyway—I didn't think anything of it if he muddled up a few things here and there. I was more concerned that this whole business with the protests was consuming him. He often sounded groggy during our phone calls, having stayed up all night in a state of hysteria. He gave up shaving. Once, when I took him a dish of leftovers, I saw a mess of blankets and a pillow on the couch in front of the TV.

In an effort to get his mind off the protests, I invited the whole family over for dinner. My father arrived first and went straight to the television and flicked on the news. My aunts arrived shortly after with a bottle of wine each. The older one had brought her son, and the younger one had brought a series of parking tickets she'd accumulated over the last four months. Her plan was to take them with her to the protests. "I can't get a judge to hear me, not even a police officer. When I go to the municipal court, I petition the secretary to speak to someone about this and they say everyone is busy, no matter how many complaints I file. Well, there are so many cops at the protests, I'll sort it out there." My aunt laughed though she wasn't joking. All the women in my family liked to carry their complaints around with them so that everyone knew their troubles.

24

The older aunt agreed with her plan, said she'd go with her if she wanted. They could go tomorrow. "I have a skirt to exchange at the mall anyway."

"I think they've cordoned off the area," I said.

"It's a protest, not a concert. They don't scan wristbands."

"I don't know," said the younger aunt. "Riot police closed down one end of my street. They made me go all the way around." She had tried to say it casually, as if to convince herself it wasn't going to be a problem, as if it was routine to have tanks and armored police at the bottom of your building. She swatted the air like dispelling cigarette smoke.

Soon after, my uncle and his wife arrived. Then, far off, as if at sea, a boom rumbled up through the flat, traveling from our feet to our knees to our stomachs. Down in the street the stray dogs started barking. My three aunts hurried over to the stereo system, attempting to conduct it. Even though, like them, it was a little dated, they couldn't figure it out at first, and they bickered until I found a bossa nova cassette and hit play. They gave me a little shove into the living room and retreated back into the kitchen, where they started doing little sashays to the music while a few steel lids rattled on bubbling pots.

In the living room, my father kept turning up the television so he could hear the news anchor, but every word the anchor said, he disagreed with. Sitting beside him were my cousin (a student of political science who had just gained admittance into a PhD program in Sweden and would be leaving at the end of the summer) and my uncle (a small-time tycoon who had recently invested in a plastics factory and just returned from a tour of meetings in China). His own son couldn't make it tonight; he was off with his friends, the children of rich oil men and real estate moguls, who all enjoyed cross-country motorcycling through the Balkans, skiing in Italy, sailing yachts in glittering regattas through the Sea of Marmara, and driving expensive cars much too fast through the snaking streets of the city.

The cousin who was here, the political science student, enjoyed teasing my father. Since the age of thirteen, he'd learned he could get a rise out of my father simply by plopping down next to him, clearing his throat, and saying, "Hey, Uncle, did you see what Erdoğan did last week?"; "Hey, Uncle, how about that Erdoğan, huh?" Today was no different. Sitting beside my father, he waited until the anchor said that good citizens needed to stay indoors for their safety, the safety of the city, and the safety of the police. Before my father could complain, my cousin nodded and said, "He's right, you know. You've got to hand it to him."

"What do little boys know?" my father shot back.

My uncle called out for pistachios and Scotch, and my aunts obliged, bringing out a little bowl of nuts and another for the shells, then a glass full to the brim with ice, then the bottle of whisky. He crunched the shells open with all these little clicking sounds, slipping the pistachios into his mouth and chewing grandly (if such a thing can be said about chewing). They rattled between his teeth as he went. He was that sort of man—impressed with himself and intent on conveying this with every aspect of his manner. Each time he lifted his glass of Scotch, he gave it a short swirl that made the ice cubes wetly clink. Another low boom, this time closer, rang out in the city. The sound was quiet yet large, felt rather than heard. My aunts shot quick glances between themselves and much too quickly went back to their dancing in the kitchen.

"All this for a tree, eh?" my uncle asked.

"A tree is never just a tree," said my cousin. "A tree is always a symbol. On its own a tree is a symbol, and a forest is wood and not a symbol."

My father told him to shut up, told the both of them to shut up. He shouted into the kitchen for my aunts to shut up though they were only dancing ("Dancing too loud!"), and he turned up the television as high as it would go, just as an anchor was talking about a renewed push by police to seize the square. Outside a red wind struck up against the windows, a host of sirens went pleading down the street, many shouts like gravel rose up in their wake. Listen to them press against the windowpane. Listen and you could hear them. In our flat, only my uncle was unafraid. We watched as something like fog formed south along the shore—more tear gas. Everywhere little clouds of tear gas sprang up in bouquets of pain, and my husband jumped out of his skin and ran straight under our bed.

Now everyone was shouting, talking to each other about anything other than the pop, pop, popping of gas canisters, talking so fast all the oxygen went out of the flat so we could hardly breathe with all the words filling up the room. My father was shouting about the 1980s, the upheavals and battles he'd listened to on the radio, the arrests and dismissals, the summary execution of fifty extremists. He talked about the military and Süleyman Demirel and Necmettin Erbakan, but these were the wrong events, the wrong actors—ghosts of a coup that had happened more than thirty years ago. I felt some gnawing desire for trouble crop up in me, and without thinking I turned to my father and asked him if he wanted to go out and watch the demonstrations to help get his bearings. I didn't know then that he was sick. I can't imagine what I would have done if he'd said yes.

He shot out of his chair and told me to shut up—something he'd never said to me, even when I was a little girl too jealous of my parents' time. My face—I must've looked like I'd just been slapped. This man telling me to shut up was not my father. I don't know now if it's a misremembering but in that moment that's all I could think: this was not my father, it was some surrogate now growling, vitriolic. I asked him what was wrong, why he was behaving this way. Instead of answering, my father started shaking his head, saying no, no, no, no. I had never seen him like this. He stomped to the television and tried to change the channel, but he'd grabbed the wrong remote and now the stereo system was blaring bossa nova, and all my relatives were asking him to turn it down, and from outside came the sounds of a protest being rent open in the sun. I kept repeating over and over: "Dad, you are not okay." He pushed the television over. It thudded awkwardly, bouncing without breaking. My cousin turned off the stereo system. My aunts came in from the kitchen. Then, sitting on the coffee table in the fresh silence, my father admitted that he didn't know where he was.

I calmed him down. No one thought much of his outburst, he was an easily excited old man, but I wasn't the sort to avoid doctors like the rest of my family. We went straightaway to his physician, who suggested a specialist, who did some scans and told us they couldn't identify the problem, and mentioned that if it had been an isolated incident, it would likely clear up on its own. "These are stressful times," they said. "I've known a patient to suddenly lose a finger from anxiety." But they didn't explain.

All my life I have been accused of an unwarranted optimism. After trying in vain to get answers from the builders about my new en suite prison cell, I figured I might as well accept life's peculiar gift to me. That afternoon, I made my father a bit of lunch and tucked him into his chair in front of the TV, then I took the car to the small storage unit we rented out of an old granary up the road. When my father moved in with us, we stuffed most of our personal belongings into boxes to make room for him, keeping only the most utilitarian items for everyday use. We had planned to rent the storage space until he recovered and we could populate our lives once more with our erstwhile possessions (*where did I put that book? have you seen the blue vase? why is the potato peeler missing?*). That's always how we put it, especially my husband: "once Dad is back to his old self," which, with Alzheimer's, only means:

"once he dies." Of course you can't say this; you don't even want to catch yourself thinking it for fear that the thought becomes an invitation.

I felt quite giddy as I gathered up all the junk in our storage unit and threw it in the back of the car. I couldn't fit everything so I made two trips, hauling boxes and fumbling with awkwardly shaped items—the large vacuum cleaner, the hallway mirror—until my fingers blistered at their joints. With everything removed, I told the manager of the rental unit to close our account. A rush of relief swept over me—just think of the money we would save not having to rent storage. My husband could hardly be upset if he found out about the prison now. He might even be proud of me when, in a few weeks' time, he noticed our bank account steadily fattening. The storage manager had me sign a few papers and said I'd have to pay for the remainder of the month, used or otherwise. They showed me the balance and I realized we would be saving hardly any money at all, certainly not enough to offset the costs of our now ruined bathroom, and yet how acutely we had felt that same monthly rent while we were paying it. That's debt, I suppose.

I lugged the extra chair and side table, a rolled-up carpet, boxes, books, kitchen appliances—all of it into the prison cell, which, though cramped, held our effects quite well, and certainly it was very secure, more secure than a granary in rural Italy. If I couldn't have a new bathroom, I'd at least get free storage out of it. As I was stacking boxes in the corner of the cell, I thought again about what would happen if my husband checked our bank account and saw that there was a mouse's portion of extra cash piling up in there. I thought up a few little lies: perhaps my father had insisted on contributing to the household budget out of his paltry retirement savings, or quite out of character I had won it during a streak of blackjack, or else I had finally found a remote, part-time, Turkish-language school psychologist position. But it was useless to worry—another builder needed hiring; a new bathroom needed installing. If anything, I would soon have to come up with an explanation for the fast disappearance of our remaining cash.

I slipped a thumb under the flap of the nearest box, releasing a thin scent. It wasn't musty or stale as one might expect, but sharp, rummaged out from under the bottom of my cerebellum. Opening the box properly, I pulled a few knickknacks out and sorted them, glad to find them in my life again. In this box were happy books; in this box were glittering picture frames; in this box were my old boots and mittens and the scarves I'd worn when we went to the mountains around Rize for our third wedding anniversary. We had planned a weeklong hiking holiday and even contemplated (though neither of us had any experience) overnighting in the forest. Our first day was an eight-hour circuit, breathtaking views of mist-mantled hills, shallow mountains with sharp gullies that went straight into the sea with little tea plantations growing down their sides. At the summit we had meze and strong tea and a mouthful each of sticky ice cream and came down pleased with our journey and the prospects of what other tranquil joys the week had in store, but the next morning our feet were so covered in blisters and boils that we stayed shacked up in our bed-and-breakfast all day. Reluctant to let all our rented equipment go to waste, my husband pitched the tent in our room while I opened the windows and scattered bread on the sills to attract birds. We guessed their names as the creatures alit, and after dark we tried spying constellations from across the room. We had sex, each of us laughing at the pain in our feet at every movement. The next morning, stepping gingerly, we took our tent down to the back garden of the guesthouse, and spent the day rubbing ice and ointments on the pads of each other's feet. That evening, after igniting all the roadside flares my husband kept in his trunk, and cooking a bit of sucuk over some coals, we tried to have sex again, laughing again, wincing at each thrust because our toes, heels, ankles, shins were on fire, but committing to it anyway, and doing so again each night until at last we had recovered and had to take our bus home.

In the same box were a few of the flares, unfired, a knapsack we'd rented, and, underneath all this, a sprinkle of soil with a small plant that had managed to grow, despite its cramped and lightless quarters, vegetal and fresh—a little tea bush somehow.

That evening, my husband came home particularly tired. A shouting match had erupted at the garage over an engine part, or maybe it had something to do with the axle. Or maybe it was neither of those and I could name only those two parts of a car. He'd misunderstood the customer, a young woman, and ended up installing or removing something unrelated to her problem. The head mechanic told her they'd rectify it, no charge, but it would take another day. I guess she had an engagement in Siena that night. She called my husband an ignorant Arab, good-for-nothing, and a few other names he had not heard before so did not know. He told her he was Turkish. His boss kicked her out of the garage and had a tow truck take her car someplace else.

"What shall we do for dinner?" he asked, which was his way of asking me what I was going to make.

"I thought potato soup. It's been chilly."

"With any . . . any . . ." He switched to Italian. "Shall we have sandwiches with it?"

When we emigrated, we had reserved our mother tongue for inside the flat and nowhere else, at first in an effort to hasten our command of Italian, but then maintained the rule, as we realized there were many Italians who couldn't hear the difference between Turkish and Arabic and who, judging by the looks, would prefer not to hear Arabic at all. My husband and I were very proud of how well our Italian had progressed (we'd been seven years in the country, after all), but recently he had been struggling to find the right words in Turkish.

I hadn't meant to reply in Italian. I was going to say *Yes, with sandwiches* in Turkish, but as I started, I found my mind inexplicably blank. I dug and dug while we carried on chatting, but no matter the depth I went, there wasn't a word of Turkish to be unearthed. It didn't seem to bother my husband that I was pausing for longer intervals, concentrating with great effort to remember such ludicrously familiar phrases as *pass the pepper*. So I continued with Italian, and so did my husband, until at last my father, grumbling as he came to join us, said in Turkish that it was too warm outside for soup and flipped a switch in my husband and me both. I loosened my grip on the wooden spoon, which I did not realize had become very tight; in fact I found my whole body had been tensed and hunching over the stove. I asked in Turkish for more pepper. My husband replied in Turkish, adding something about the garage. We ate our dinner, and then I walked my father to his bedroom, pulling the blanket up to his neck though he kept pulling it back down; all the while I was thinking about an article I had read years before in a general psychology newsletter. As we learn a new language, it explained, we become a different person. As we access different linguistic structures, our personalities shift: to reflect the different concepts available to us through different words, but also because of the new company we keep in a new language, and because of our preconceived notions about the language—all these things alter who we become under it.

In Italian, I have become a more buoyant person. I know the words for *happy*, *nice*, *beautiful*, *joyful*, *kind*, *generous*, *love*, *warmth*, but I never did much to learn all the branching synonyms of *bad*, that large, dark canopy. In language lessons, everyone starts with "It is a beautiful day"; "That is a nice dress"; "You have pretty teeth." For a long time, I just used the negative: not beautiful, not nice, not pretty. Everything was in relation to the good, badness marked only by good's absence. I'd lost that melancholic language I had grown so reliant upon in Turkish. I felt superficial at times. I suppose that was why, after emigrating, I began to enjoy classical music, jazz, even movie scores. Language is a fickle, feeble pathway. When it retreats from us, what means remain for revealing ourselves to others? Music without lyrics. Film without dialogue. Paintings without subjects. Am I less of a person, the fewer words I have in my pocket? Or am I simply shallower?

I asked my husband if he loved me.

"I love you," he said. "Of course."

"How do you know?"

"What does that mean?"

"We're speaking Italian."

"The sun is outside. So what?"

"I'm not the same."

"We are always the same," he said. "Winter, summer; in the shower, in the car."

"I'm not the same," I told him. If it was like putting on a new skin to speak in a different language, if it was so easy to become a new person, didn't we need to make our vows again in Italian? What if he didn't really love the Italian me, or what if I didn't truly love the Italian him? Shouldn't we need to rediscover each other, to settle in, to injure each other all over again? Shouldn't we need to become ourselves once more, and in the process compare what has been gained and lost?

"Well, okay. I love you anyway," he said.

When had it last struck me that I should miss Turkey? My father's needs kept me constantly preoccupied and generally avoidant of introspection, but more than that, it never felt to me that I had left Turkey—rather it had abandoned me. We brushed our teeth and went to bed very early, and I cried because I had not known how irreparable my separation from Istanbul had been until now, until this trick of speech left me briefly mute—scraping, scraping, scraping at the bottom of myself for any word at all, ripping up the floorboards and digging under the coils and spools of muscles deep under the skin and finding nothing.

My father seemed to regain a great deal of normalcy after the Gezi Park protests. Sure, he forgot a few things here and there. Generally, though, they were mistakes rather than conspicuous gaps—*I called you yesterday, not last week; we had breakfast together just this morning.* I tried not to read too much into it, as if he were a toddler who had accidentally knocked over our TV: it's not a life sentence to delinquency. Nor was my father's memory so bad. Certainly no one else was worried about it, and I tried to borrow a bit of their unconcern. I started keeping track of my own hiccups of memory as a way to diminish my fears about my father. I'd never remembered to get everything at the supermarket, even with a list. I would drive a car until the warning light came on beside the fuel gauge, then forget the next morning that I'd run out of gas. It calmed me down to think this way. Nobody was perfect.

I regret doing this, making it out to be an episode rather than the start of him dying. He was still very lucid, so lucid it wasn't even a question yet. He was clever and quick and humorous. He called me a lot. He asked about my work, the children I tested. He was happier than he had been for years. Since my mother died, he had retreated into himself. He was quite a bit younger than her; I assumed they must have talked about it, the prospect of her dying first. I know my husband and I talk about which of us will die first. But she died so young. Not even fifty years old. No amount of talking means anything when it's unexpected. It crippled him, though who am I to say I was much better?

Yet after the protests, he was laughing, laughing, quite unlike himself. After our visit to the doctor and the scans, he was jubilant to a degree I had never seen him before. It was a disconcerting tone now entering our lives; not that we were an unhappy family, but certainly an uneasy one, riddled with nerves in our own ways—young widows and widowers were perhaps a little too common when one looked at my family tree. I hadn't thought of it then, but later I wondered if the memory of my mother had begun falling away from him already.

The next day my father tried to make himself a bit of lunch as I cleaned the flat. Sometimes, he mustered up a bit of his old self and went about pretending as if all was well (or maybe, gruesomely, he wasn't pretending at all and was just gone). He was childlike in the way he interacted with the objects around him. He sat me down and said, "Lunch," while pointing to a big bowl of salad on the table. I took a bite and spat it out, which didn't bother him. He did the same, spitting it all over the table with a smile, though maybe he was only mimicking me. Instead of dressing it with olive oil, he had used whiskey. Half a bottle of whiskey, gone. I told him to clear the table so I could go back to cleaning. He grabbed the salt shaker, but upside down, and walked back to the kitchen and then to the bathroom with it, putting it in the medicine cabinet and scattering a path of salt behind him. These were the worst days because he was active. It was hard to ignore him when he got out of his chair and puttered about. When he sat still and watched television, he was more like a stuffed animal or delicate vase, and could do me no harm.

After making sure he had a bowl of oatmeal and his medications, after taking him for a short walk around the apartment and tucking him into his big chair, I told him that I loved him.

"I believe you," he whispered.

"I mean it."

"I believe you."

"You don't recognize me," I said.

"I believe you!" he shouted.

Before I had a chance to think about it, I found myself running, running away from my father, heading for my bedroom, where I usually hid away, and I was now lifting the tarp to the bathroom, and slipping under it, and crawling into the prison, my movements strangely silent, no echo coming back from the concrete walls. I started talking to myself, just to hear something; I felt the shallow vibrations of speech in my own throat, but nothing seemed to come out. I heard nothing for a long time, as if my head had been stuffed into a down pillow. I moved the boxes around, tidying up to keep myself occupied. I bent and hoisted, grunting periodically to check on my strange deafness. I slid a few of them under the bed and the table in the cell to hide them from quick glances, then tucked the rest by the toilet behind the modesty partition. The cell felt full of air, somehow, so completely stuffed with air that I could swallow a big gulp, could take long, never-ending gulps of it. My slippered feet made shushing sounds across the floor, and the quieter tickings of the cell started to resound in my ears. Another breath, another breath—fresh, calmed at last.

Then the guard came by in his mustache. "What is all of this?"

"It's a few of my things."

"You can't have things."

"Sure I can. Prisoners can have things."

"Not in this prison. This is for very dangerous criminals, so cunning they might turn a pipe cleaner into a weapon or a washcloth into a lockpick or a water bottle into a bomb, and you've got an entire household in there!"

"I'm not clever enough to turn a washcloth into a bomb," I said.

"A water bottle. Don't be ridiculous."

"It's just a few boxes. There's no harm in a book or a—" He saw the chair and the rolled-up carpet behind the low partition.

"What is happening here? Oh no, you can't! I said don't cause a ruckus, and what is this if not a bona fide ruckus, my god!"

"I haven't done anything," I said. "I've just rearranged the furniture."

"There isn't supposed to be any furniture. But don't say any more. I don't want to know it. I want to be able to say: 'I don't know anything.' All my life, this is all I wanted to say. All through my school years, I studied and worked so hard to be able to say 'I don't know anything,' and look at you coming around to ruin it."

An effervescent and ticklish happiness gripped me. Turkish! I was speaking Turkish—and with a stranger to boot! Immediately I felt warmed and comforted, and though I was securely trapped inside a prison, I felt I could taste the hints of brine and juniper trees in the air, and I wanted to swallow up this sensation, eat it ungingerly.

The guard stormed off, but I begged him to come back, to talk with me, to shout anything at me, to tell me where he was from. I pressed my face into the gap between two bars, squeezed my cheeks against them. I shouted down the hall: "Please, mister watchman, come back and tell me about your neighborhood!"—whether it was one of those quiet squares on the fringes of the city; or if it was in an apartment complex on the high streets of Istanbul; or if it was provincial, with peasant faces flashing at the windows. North of the city, along the coast, there are tumbledown houses and sheds standing in their huddles. You can see them with binoculars during pleasure cruises down the Bosporus. As you come in from the Black Sea, the city reveals itself in gradients of hills pouring into the water. Peel back this layer to see Bebek—now Arnavut-köy, now Kuruçeşme—all green with white houses, like marble stairs down their hillsides. Some days the water is thick and dark as velvet; other days, it is flat and bright in the sun, and other days still it is a quicksilver sardine in a shallow inlet, and in the faltering dusk I have seen it burn like copper, and in the misty mornings it vanishes and the city teeters above a void. I could almost see the hills of the old city, fat with ancient domes bubbling over them, and, closer, the slender, prickly tips of minarets—and now in my prison cell I felt cold and wet, I was sucked out of my daydream to find the floor drowned in briny water. I laughed, and the water gathered its skirts into bunches and twirled at my ankles, and I was terrified. I shouted to the guard: "Something is happening to my room!" And the water turned inscrutably dark and I could see a cloud bank gathering on the ceiling, and I could feel now the coarse, stony beach of Istanbul at my feet, my toes curling around its pebbles. I shouted again for the guard: "Help, I will drown!" and it was filling up now with more water, pike and sea bream, eels and gulls, and now a fisherman's pole and line, and the far-off peal of a ferry horn, and the scent of fresh expectancy, and the silver of Istanbul under a bracing and pleasant rain. I threw open the door to my bedroom, hurrying to close out the flood, but when I retrieved my hair dryer for my wet clothes, I found everything was dry already and nothing as it should be.

I must have gone too long without food, or maybe I was dehydrated, and imagined everything. Well, yes, I had imagined everything, it was a daydream after all, but I did not know of any daydreams that were in the habit of slipping out of the mind and becoming real. I missed Istanbul. That was how I explained it. You'll believe anything when you need comfort. But how then did my husband, that night as I tried very hard to fall asleep without success, pull a small seashell (still with a bit of gritty mud in its aperture) from my hair and hold it up to the darkness like an answer?

Maybe I was foolish, but it caught me by surprise when my husband discovered the prison in our bathroom. He became a whirlwind through the house, knocking over the lamps, a side table, all of my father's medical apparatus. He stuffed a few items into a hard-shell suitcase—his unfinished crossword puzzles, the tea bags, the toaster, a few paintbrushes and paints, his watch and trousers, but mostly loads of underwear, every pair. Before I could say a word to him, he flew out of the flat, crashing down the staircase in a bunch of thuds like an awkward drumroll.

It was a half hour or so later—enough time that my husband could have feasibly ran to the train station, checked the timetables, waited in the queue, bought a ticket, and boarded a train bound for Milan or Turin and then out of Italy altogether—when I was just saying to myself I was now husbandless and alone, that jumping through the door came my husband again, his face fat with dread, saying "What are you doing? Aren't you coming too?"

I laughed (perhaps from shame or some other feeling that lies buried in our soils) and pulled him by the arm into the flat, though I didn't embrace him, as I might have liked. I sat him down on the couch next to me and took his hands in mine. He must've only got halfway to the station, a mess of worries zooming through his mind, when he realized I wasn't following him and darted back home.

"We can't stay."

"Why not?" I asked. I don't know why I said it. He wasn't wrong, and I wasn't a particularly argumentative person. I was only now becoming aware of my resignation to the situation. I had abandoned any attempt to fix this debacle, though really how would I have done that, anyway? Certainly I had tried; I had given it a go. Is it right to say *resignation* about all this? It felt more like the rush of falling in a dream, the effervescent adrenaline of that moment that stretches out indefinitely, intoxicatingly, just before you wake.

"You're being purposefully obtuse, I see. Or is something else the matter?"

"Just sit down and listen for a minute."

He refused. If the Turkish government found out we had part of their prison in our flat, they'd arrest us. I tried to argue that we wouldn't be extradited, but he countered that they wouldn't need to bother about that, they could let themselves into our flat through the cell and march us right into prison. He reminded me that we had been driven out of the country, that Turkey wanted us dead or worse. He said that this must have been some new development by the Interior Ministry to hunt down political enemies. He said my father was in no condition to be in jail. He said I wouldn't like it much either. He said these things as if I didn't know them too.

"Please, just listen to me," I said. "Just give it a little while. Everything will be fine." I regretted saying that, because I had to admit nothing about this felt like it would turn out well for us, and yet I couldn't help wanting to stay put.

"Oh no, no. I can't do this. I have to leave, and quickly. What about my acid? I have to go before my ulcer . . ." And he was gone.

PART II

THIS MORNING, I ASKED my dad to be ready early. We had to go to the pharmacy to pick up more memantine. It's reserved for severe symptoms—what none of the doctors call late-stage symptoms. Everything was referred to in gradients of severity rather than time. I get it. It was hard to apply a timeline to certain diseases, certain symptoms. That's the thought in everyone's mind, though: time. They wouldn't say to me that they think my father has at best six months left. They wouldn't say to me that I should prepare. I appreciated that at least. As if the last decade hadn't been a preparation, as if my current life wasn't just some liminal existence at the skirt of my father's funeral march. But he's lived this long. By a miracle, he's lived eight years and done so well for most of it. Imagine the paradox of this existence: he is dying, so certainly he might as well be considered dead already, it will happen as surely as pigeons shit on freshly washed cars, but there's no saying when. You can't mark it down on the calendar and put your life predictably, if inconveniently, on hold. It is slow, slow, slow as tectonic plates in their grand shifts. What do I do next to this? What do I do, standing on the lip of this suffering and mortality, frailty and vulnerability, in order to keep myself sane? How am I expected not to change? How am I supposed to escape this unscarred?

In the brain, a neuron has to receive a strong enough stimulus to trip its threshold and trigger a voltage change in order to fire, shooting the voltage shift down the line. Often it won't receive enough stimulus and so the electrical chain peters out—failed initiations. Each day felt like the stimulus that would trigger something in me, but it never did. My threshold jumped just out of reach each time, and I was left building the charge. It grew and grew without firing. All this grief collided with other particles of grief unreleased. The threshold is pushed back each day because it is time to wake up and dress my father and make him some food and make myself a bit of food too and there isn't time to cry. They didn't have a pamphlet about that in the doctor's office. They didn't have a pamphlet with a handy little title like: *Hurry Up and Die So I Can Begin Mourning You.*

Anyway, I'd told him to get ready early, knowing I couldn't leave him on his own. "When your alarm goes off, put on your trousers and your sweater."

He nodded at me, a bit sharper than usual, and I took that to mean he understood.

I told him again: "Trousers, sweater," pointing at them.

"Yes, yes. Sweater. Trousers."

This morning, I found him in his pajamas watching the countryside in the window. By then I did not have time to dress him so he went with me in his pajamas. The pharmacist asked if we had any questions.

"Is there ravioli?" Dad asked.

"What's that?"

"Nothing," I said.

"If he has a question, I have to hear it before I give you the medication."

I sighed. Where is the mercy in requiring a lucid conversation with a dementia patient before they can get their drugs? "He asked if there was ravioli," I translated.

The pharmacist didn't blush or smile or even seem to register this non sequitur. "There is good ravioli across the street, actually. I eat there all the time. They might require pants."

I didn't like this pharmacist. I paid the nine euros and guided my father back through the aisles. He put all his weight on my arm though he had his cane in his other hand.

Memantine is only prescribed when there's little left to preserve. "At best," said the neurologist, "he'll be able to use the bathroom on his own for a few more months."

Before my husband left, before the prison, even before the renovation began, I had become my father's caretaker. There were a lot of reasons for this: because I am a woman; because he is *my* father; because in Italy my husband found a job first; because I had two heaps extra of patience in me compared to most people—but the main reason, though it was never spoken, was because I had worked in a hospital back in Istanbul. Of course, I was a specialist in childhood development, not a doctor or nurse. I was a psychologist, which ironically was the last sort of doctor my father needed, though everyone always noted how lucky he was to have an expert of the brain for a daughter. I was never the lucky one in these statements. And I never pointed out that what he needed was a neurologist and a physical therapist more than me. At most I could have helped the people around him process their emotional responses to his jarring temper changes, but I was the only person around him, and though I didn't hold his fits against him, everything has its toll. Now I was in a foreign country, swimming on the floor of the ocean without bones made for all the pressure.

In the first few days after my husband's departure I was relieved. The prison would have been incredibly difficult to hide day in and day out for who knew how long. I needed to reattach the P trap to my father's sink (until now I had just let it dump into a bucket I kept in the cabinet). I could give up phoning the contractor, who by now had surely blocked my number anyway. I could clean up the mess in the bedroom. And best of all, I wouldn't need to navigate my husband's anxiety in the midst of all this. Yes, of course I was disappointed he'd gone. I loved him very much, but he wasn't the sort of person whose company you sought in the middle of a crisis. He knew this much about himself as well. It wasn't that he loafed around without any purpose. His work at the garage—repetitious lifting and jerking, stretching and bending, fine and constant articulations of his vise-strong fingers—swiftly tired him compared to his desk work back in Turkey. He worked hard, but away from the house and technically in service to others, whereas I worked always for the two of us (or three of us), cooking, cleaning, shopping, scheduling, planning, making small repairs. His departure turned out to be a practical solution to a great many problems, but of course, it came with its own burdens. For example, we had lost our only income overnight. I'd need to get work somewhere soon.

Let's pretend that's easy, though, and I find a job—what was I supposed to do with my father all day while I'm out? He couldn't stay alone; there were too many sharp corners in the flat. I could have hired a nurse, or home hospice specialist, but I'd looked before and that cost at least eighty euros a day, plus a maid or a cook occasionally so that the fridge was full and the rooms were tidy. Nine euros here, eighty euros there, a new cane every other week because he kept leaving them places and forgetting—it added up when your pension was left behind in another country. All the money I'd make would just feed into paying my replacement, meaning I'd need to work longer hours, which would require more people paid to visit my father and take care of him. At least rents were low in our village. That was part of the reason we had chosen it: I had seen (in fact, a friend of mine showed me) an article online about the rampant emptying of Italian, Spanish, and French countrysides. To combat this, some Italian villages had taken to paying foreigners to settle there. "Is this the same Italy that sends back refugee boats?" I had asked and we both darkly laughed. I didn't read much of the article and never followed up with any government agencies to take advantage, so like chumps we were paying to exist when it could've been free, but it was still cheaper than most of the rest of the EU.

In short, I had about three months to find work before my father and I began living off saltine crackers and jelly, and four months, maybe five, before the utilities were turned off and we would go hungry—just in time for my father to start uncontrollably shitting himself, if you could take the word of a neurologist. I started looking that evening.

My aunts called. They always used one of those encrypted apps that advertise their reluctance to cooperate with governments. They did this in part because it was free to call that way, though I knew they also nurtured a dollop of suspicion that they were being watched. Half the country had switched from standard messaging apps as more and more people were arrested on the basis of texts they had sent and received. It was difficult to keep track of what could land you in trouble, what inane messages could be construed as treason. One day you're living life as blissfully as anyone else, the next you're brought into the police station, your phone subpoenaed, and you're giving a deposition about reservations you made at a restaurant with some friends six weeks ago. Dozens of Turks were sued by the government for insults against the president every day. No one was exempt—there were frequently stories of children being pulled in for questioning after posting jokes in chat forums or sending their friends pictures of poop and naming the poops Erdoğan. Not that using WhatsApp really protected you, but I didn't bother mentioning that to my aunts.

In a well-maintained routine, my aunts had been calling me for years on specific dates. I could expect them to call on May Day and Republic Day in October; one day usually right in the middle of Ramazan; on my birthday, my husband's birthday, my father's birthday, and the day before their own birthdays, so that they could complain I had not called them to wish them well, and when I reminded them that they were a day early they would say, "Well, you're out of the country, the time difference, we thought . . ." as if I wasn't just an hour behind them. I could also expect a call around the anniversary of my mother's death, though never on the exact date—that was a void, as if calling me on her death-day was the same as invoking her, something they never did. "Just checking up on you," is what they said, and we never mentioned my mother at all in these calls, only the incredibly small trials of the day ahead of us: peeling back the strings on pea pods because they catch in the gaps between my teeth; investigating why an open car door prevents the headlights from shutting off; listening to the doorman talk about his decrepit vegetable garden the whole elevator ride.

They always rang off by saying they missed me but without asking when I would come back. They didn't broach the subject of a return, no matter how short. They didn't ask if I would like them to visit me in Italy either; they didn't mention all the sights very nearby to us that they had wanted to see: Pompeii, Capri, Amalfi. To begin with, it was probably much safer for them to go on living estranged from my father and me. Were we to turn up and get through customs and put down their address as our residence, it could mean a fine, loss of unemployment benefits, even a prison sentence. They didn't have to say this to me. I knew well enough—it was a risk to have dubious characters for relations. Secondly, if I still knew my aunts at all, they avoided discussing any sort of reunion because they quite enjoyed their distance from my father's declining health. If they came here, there would be no avoiding him. Worse, I might ask them directly for help, and they'd (rightly) feel obligated to assist. They'd have to take an intimate role in all the grotesque rituals of decay they could so easily ignore from across the sea. People think the heartbreak of dementia comes when your loved ones look at you with that bank of unrecognition built over their faces, but for me it struck sharpest in the moments when I realized I had changed roles with my father so completely, so basely, that I had become the person who cleaned the shit off him, in that diabolical rhyme of ageing. Of course my aunts did not wish to be reunited with their brother. Who would invite themselves into this torture by choice? When we envisioned our family gatherings, on the agenda were cocktail hours by the sea, afternoon tea, long nights of tavla, and early coffees in some alley under the influence of Galata Tower. Not on the agenda: bedsores, aggressive and hostile outbursts, blood clots, piss stains, pneumonia, sepsis.

I couldn't understand why they had called that night, which was none of the usual dates, until the older one mentioned my cousin. He had just finished his PhD and gotten engaged, and they were planning a reception to celebrate. I told them they should hold the celebration at a restaurant we used to go to for conspicuous events in the family.

"What restaurant?"

"It's overlooking the Bosporus," I said.

"What good restaurant isn't?" she said, which was an exaggeration; in fact many of them were losing their views to changing skylines and new developments.

"It's got a view of the bridge."

"Which bridge?"

I tried to remember the name of the restaurant. I told her it had formerly operated as a school or municipal building, or something else that would have wings and corridors. It had a patio, and umbrellas, and a stone balustrade.

"My darling, you are saying this as if there is only one restaurant we visit," the younger aunt said.

We really did hardly dine anywhere else, not all together anyway. "No, no, for birthdays, for celebrations. Regularly, I mean."

"Can I—"

"They have white tablecloths, and waiters in ties—"

"Can I ask a question?" my aunt interrupted.

"I don't remember if the food is any good, but—"

"Can I ask a question?"

"Of course," I said.

"I've never been there," said my aunt.

It came clearly to me then—the restaurant was in an

old palace that had, after the foundation of the Republic, been converted into a girl's lycée. "One of you attended it, or was it Hala that did? She went to finishing school, right?"

"Maybe."

"It has an enormous patio," I said. "The front drive has a double staircase."

"I've never been on a patio."

I closed my eyes and imagined driving in a compact car up a winding street no wider than the car itself. Katy Perry was on the radio. The street was cobbled. The houses around us were white. We pulled into a small courtyard and a valet took the keys. I was about to say all this, trying to remember a smell, when my aunts said they had to go. They sent their love to my father and my husband. I sent mine to the rest of my aunts, my uncle, my cousins. I was sending more love, since they were all over there, but cleverly, my aunts started sending love to people in Istanbul I had been closer to in order to make up for this gulf. We sent our love to relatives neither had heard from in many months, we sent our love to friends, to neighbors, to pet cats and pet birds, and refugees of every nation, and eventually we sent love and fortune to everyone on both sides of the sea, and we hung up.

I had two pictures of the restaurant that had survived all the phone upgrades, different cloud servers, inbox clearouts. I couldn't find them right away but I knew they existed. I used to look at them regularly, when we first moved, not because they were the most striking images I had of Istanbul, but because they were the last I took in the city. We had gone for cocktails as a family, as the whole family. It was a send-off but no one acknowledged that, no one mentioned that the next morning my husband, my father, and I were going to leave. We'd spent the previous month pawning or selling all our largest, heaviest possessions that were too expensive to ship overseas, and packing everything else into boxes and suitcases. To prevent a somber evening from falling, I had suggested this restaurant with the patio, this place of so many happy memories, hoping that its happiness might rub off on our impending and indefinite exile. Unfortunately, the effort had backfired, and now marring my memories of this terrace were our stifled and trite conversations of that evening, pretending not to think about the next day and the next and the next, all cascading down over us into one long night.

But the two pictures I took that afternoon miraculously escaped the tense atmosphere of the gathering. I had looked at these pictures every day for probably a whole year—I must have; they were my desktop wallpaper and my phone background, respectively. They were happy pictures. Quotidian, yes, but all the more immortal for it, immortal in their tranquility.

I went through the flat looking for them, starting with my phone of course, and finding that the oldest picture in it was only from last year. At the end of the phone's image gallery was an unchronological jumble of pictures of prescription bottles, a few plates of food, and finally two pictures of printed photographs of my mother with her sisters when they were young. Next, I grabbed my laptop, but something about the cloud synchronization had confused the filing system on the computer itself, filling it with duplicates and triplicates of documents I'd only used once, along with many dead-end, empty folders for things that had been (if the labels were any indicator) actually quite important. I checked my email the same way, sifting through the messages I'd sent myself and finding only scans of my passport, a few immigration documents, a birth certificate, and my husband's anxiety medication prescription. Then I remembered I had bought an external hard drive a few years back, and so I went about the house trying to find it, or else find my old laptop that had, in its obsolescence, slowed so much it was little more than a paperweight. I rummaged through all the junk drawers (there were many, that's the type of people my husband and I were), the spare cupboards, the backs of closets, the loose baseboard of the kitchen, under my bed and even under my father's bed, but there was nothing. All the time I had been searching, I had been trying in vain to remember what the restaurant actually looked like. The missing pictures were so completely familiar to me, and yet, as I tried to imagine them, tried to see either one of them in my mind's eye, they appeared porous, distorted by a mist that reduced them to a series of indistinguishable features, like a dream that is full only of the notions of recognizable images, rather than the images themselves. I worked myself almost into a frenzy, wanting to remember something, anything, needing right now to hold in my hands the past, the past, the past, and this was it, a definitive place and time, monumental in my life; there was evidence, but where?

"What is it, what is it?" my father growled from the doorway, finding me curled halfway under his bed and sneezing from the dust.

I asked him if he knew the name of the restaurant. At least then I could look it up on the internet and see pictures and build up its image in my mind part by part— where it is, what they serve, what I drank and ate and how I laughed and in what direction I was looking trying not to feel sad, trying not to feel anything at all.

"It's not correct," he said, pointing at me on the ground.

"Oh, stop it."

"It's not—"

"That's enough."

"You get out," he said. "I can't stand you. I can't stand here."

"Stop it, Dad."

His whole body gave a twitch from head to toe— momentarily overcome by revulsion—and then his face became placid, his weight fell onto his cane. "Dad," I said again. He knew the restaurant, of course he did, he must remember it, we went so often. I wanted to coax it out of him, but I could see he was gone from the room now, he was trapped somewhere else. He had drifted off the earth into the dark chasm of dementia that erases a person so completely from being. In that moment, it felt like all of Istanbul was retreating, along with my father, into this abyss.

The boxes in my prison cell! I hadn't thought to check them for an old laptop or phone or flash drive that would have my two pictures. At once I was in the cell, rifling through my possessions, practically tipping them out in my eagerness to investigate every box. I found a sewing kit, coupons years expired, notepads and pens, pairs of scissors—a junk box. I tossed it aside and grabbed the next, but it was heavy and I didn't have the right grip. It fell, and two candelabras clattered to the floor. I grabbed the next box and turned it upside down; old bedspreads and pillows flopped out. Box after box I dumped onto the floor, unworried about the racket, unworried about the guard.

Here came all these memories falling like leaves around me: the restaurant was my mother's favorite place in the whole city; it had been a finishing school, yes, her mother had attended it, and also one of her sisters (but which one?), and my mother, watching her sister leave each morning, had come to covet the school, wishing to join in the classes, especially the table-setting lessons, the etiquette of meals; my mother, while I was in knee socks, had covered our low coffee table with a white bedsheet, and laid two immaculate settings for tea—hers and mine, each with a name card—and told me this was exactly what my aunt had done with her after school when she was in knee socks herself, this sister had come straight home and, wanting to show off her new manners, hosted high tea with my mother, showing her, slowly, the turn of a hand at the proper moment, the sensitive and minutely tender slip of a butter knife across a plane of toast or a teaspoon into a sugar cellar; my mother giggled through our finger sand-wiches, gossiping about my toys, and I giggled with her, enchanted now by the tradition of the finishing school and its part in our family history and wanting to enroll myself, though the school had closed down; she tickled me now under my chin, now at my cheeks, and clumsily I mim-icked her—instead of tickling grabbing her cheeks and pulling them wide, pulling them to make her squinched eyes even wider, and the two of us were a thing and its small mirror, wide smiling faces.

I don't remember if she told me then that it had re-opened as a restaurant, or if that only happened a few years later, but in the mind a memory takes no time at all. The process of remembering felt active, creative in fact. It felt like I was constructing the memories out of the vibrant and grotesque materials of thought. It felt like I was a ves-sel being filled. The pair of us were excited about the res-taurant, having built up our expectations of its elegance and refinement. Our first trip had been a gorgeously clan-destine affair; with a quick finger to the lips, she said we wouldn't even invite Dad, we would have an afternoon for princesses, just the two of us. I don't remember much be-yond this spirit of secrecy (no doubt exaggerated for my benefit, the way parents like to draw their children into affectionate duplicities) and how all future visits to the res-taurant felt shrouded in the same good-natured mystery. But where, where were the pictures?

They were both taken on the patio, in that restaurant in the hills overlooking the Bosporus, one recording the faces of all the relatives, the other facing the water. It was a beautiful view, and everything, from the cocktail glasses to the breeze, felt delicate—the light gray paving stones, the carved balustrades, the wooden deck chairs, white-linened tables, the gaslights on their thin lampposts. The patio itself was more of a grand balcony built over a steep slope; a few steps down from it was a wide terrace with an immaculately cropped lawn, and below this the tangle of coast pines and hillside houses all the way to the sea. There was no one in the first photo except for my aunts and uncle on one side of the long table, and a waiter in his black waistcoat and tie delivering a tray of drinks. The sun was behind low, thin clouds, making everything silver and catching on all the metal objects: the silverware, the sun-glass frames, the bracelets and thin necklaces—turning them white. All the other tables in the image were empty. In the other picture, the one that looked out to the sea, there were two strangers, a German couple sitting at the table ahead of us, older and tan. They were silent, watching the tankers and yachts weave over the water. In the photo their plates were empty, the water goblets frosted with condensation and catching the light in a way that made you feel thin and hollow looking at it, everything giving the impression of fragility.

My friend Lucia did not answer her phone, nor did her husband, Giovanni, at first. I kept calling them each in turn until at last Giovanni picked up, breathless, saying he was at the gym. I hung up; how silly but I had panicked. I didn't really know what I wanted to say. I could have told him hello I missed them we needed to get together again soon, very soon, urgently soon—no nothing was wrong, nothing new anyway, but things were worse without being worse, reality felt denser I guess, teeming with inertia, and also that I was completely fine. But hearing Giovanni answer, all of this jumped out of my mind—how would I explain my husband's flight, my new prison cell? I wouldn't know where to begin and he certainly would not believe me anyway. Lucia then called me, frantically saying that Gian worried something was wrong with me.

"Why do you wait, huh, why do you wait to call?" she said. "What is wrong? What is wrong that you take so long to call me, huh? I see my neighbor every day, the ugly bum, my sister too, but not you! Why does my friend take so long to call me?"

"Nothing's wrong," I said.

"We must see you. Too long. I'm sorry we canceled dinner. Come over tonight, both of you."

"We—"

"Yes, yes, all three of you in fact!"

I shouldn't have called them, should've stayed shuttered up in my odd predicament until I had things figured out. I thought about letting someone else cook for me, cook for my father too, letting someone else handle the evening while I sat absentmindedly at a table or in front of a television, mouth slightly ajar, almost drooling.

"We can't tonight but I must see you soon."

"Oh, darling, I must see you too, the decorator in the office has ruined everything. And you know about my sister, huh, and what a lot of problems I have, but you're just the sort to help me. Every time I tell Dilara a problem somehow it is solved."

This was true in a sense, but not because I ever offered help or advice—Lucia was the kind of person who was most self-possessed when pretending to solicit the opinions of others.

"Next week?" I said.

"Yes. Gian will pick up veal cutlets. I have a new pan from Switzerland to try out, though do the Swiss make good pans? Clocks, yes, all the moving parts. How many parts are in a cooking pan? All the bells and whistles—if there aren't any bells or whistles on my pan, I'll return it . . ."

It was difficult to wrangle her now, most of our phone calls went this way, and though I normally found it exhausting or at best idiosyncratic, I felt exhilarated talking to her then, planning to see her and Gian, if only because it was a normal thing to do, absolutely banal and therefore somehow sacred to me now. We blew kisses goodbye and hung up, Lucia still talking when I pressed the button.

Friends were scarce for us in Italy. A few neighbors had been kind, or else on our holidays we sometimes met tourists we liked but would never see again. Having a dependent father didn't exactly help. Over the years, as his deterioration, almost contagiously, deteriorated our own lives, my husband and I found ourselves with only one couple with whom we could reliably socialize. We met them through my husband. Giovanni had a little roadster from the sixties that he brought into the garage frequently so he could talk the ears off the mechanics. My husband loved the car and always listened intently to Gian's rambling lectures, partly because listening to Italian required an active bit of participation on his end. Then when COVID hit and everything shut down, I'm not sure whether Giovanni pitied my husband, the out-of-work immigrant, or if he simply missed his time in the garage chatting about nothing and everything, but during lockdown he called my husband over to look at the car, pretended it needed an oil change or a new filter, then chatted about this and that, always one of them inside the car and one outside so as not to catch the virus.

As I've said, my husband is quite the hypochondriac (we can't watch medical dramas because he always comes down with the same things as the patients), so the pandemic really was eating at the hem of his sanity. His time with Giovanni went a long way to mellow him, giving him a task and keeping his mind off his own mortality. So much for him, but because of my father's health we took extra precautions pushing the envelope of diligence and broaching lunacy. It meant whenever he returned from Giovanni's we spent two weeks in separate beds so that I wouldn't catch something and give it to my father. We went out dressed in a makeshift hazmat costume to fetch my father in his own costume for dinner. We became like three monks staring at each other in our cell imagining a world outside the monastery.

After the first bout of lockdowns, when everyone was crawling back out from under their rocks and workers began to protest their lost wages, Giovanni asked my husband to bring me along with him. "Surely your wife likes cars too," he said over the phone. "And if not, she can commiserate with mine about all the grease stains on our clothes."

Giovanni and his wife, Lucia, practically grabbed us by the collars and jockeyed us into their house for a long, generous dinner followed by bitters followed by espresso and then even a little bit of syrupy baklava they had ordered especially from their favorite bakery in an effort to make us feel welcomed. My husband gave me a short look that meant he felt patronized each time we were served baklava in Italy, but I pinched his thigh. I didn't feel patronized. I was enamored with Lucia and Giovanni—the latter had even learned a bit of mechanic's Turkish (the steering wheel, the axle, the clutch) to better talk with my husband about his car.

They were warm people, especially Lucia, despite how much she loved to complain, how particular and high-maintenance she seemed at first. She moaned all night that the baker had used honey instead of syrup for the baklava. "That makes it Greek, isn't that right?" And she was upset with her cook, who had not prepared the lasagna in time, forcing her to quickly pull together a pot of tortellini.

Giovanni told stories of his time as an amateur racer, and how he'd met Lucia on his father's yacht. "I wasn't serious about his old man," said Lucia, defending herself. "He was a good gift-giver." They switched as narrators with each story, sometimes fabricating things entirely; at least I had assumed as much—their lives were so foreign to me, and so far away from my routine of boiling potatoes for my father, spending hours on the phone between doctors and pharmacists who neglected to cross-check medications, or pestering overworked nurses. "It must be hard," said Giovanni. "All this, I mean," and he swept his hand over his head. "You could use a vacation, I think."

"You must come with us to Torino," said Lucia, and I knew right then, no matter how much we protested about the cost, just by her speaking this invitation it would be impossible for us to decline. "Do you ski? The Alps are something else. They have mountains in Turkey, I know, but they don't have the Alps. Skiing is a dream of course, but the most important is the après-ski. It'll be hard, no one is open, and you can't get the housekeepers to work these days, but I can manage." And she could. Lucia had a way of turning a meager and cobwebbed pantry into a sprawling cocktail party.

In the week since my husband ran off, I had caught myself, during my father's particularly disconcerting and taxing moods, stealing away into my prison cell. I would poke my head into the cell like a squirrel checking for hawks. Then I'd walk up to the bars right away and quickly return to my door, repeating this ritual three or four times before standing stock-still, hands in my pockets, in the center of the cell hearing the tightly packed emptiness. I hadn't seen the guard for days. Where had he gone? And what lay at the end of the corridor? Eventually my curiosity would be dispelled by a scrape of fear across my shoulder blades—I knew I was tempting fate in there, inviting some terrible consequence, some permanent entrapment, some trick of the prison that would see my bathroom door lock from the other side—and the thought sent me scrambling back home, but come the evening, or maybe first thing the next day, I'd be at it again. I still didn't understand why it was here, but increasingly I found the cell was just what I needed. Whenever I felt overwhelmed by my tasks—organizing and administering my father's medications; washing him, then his clothes and bedding, then cleaning the flat; my job search (which had so far amounted to little more than typing the word *jobs* into a search engine while I slowly fished the last few olives from the bottom of their jar)—whenever I couldn't concentrate on fixing up my resume or relearning how to write a letter of interest, I crept to the comforting quiet of my prison.

I did worry sometimes about the admittedly unlikely possibility of my father stumbling into my room, crawling under the tarp, and walking into the prison. Though maybe it would be normal for him, the way his thoughts had muddled—sometimes, just after finishing up dinner at the table, he walked to the window and saw the hills over Salerno and took them to be the hills of Istanbul. It's natural enough to a dementia-addled man to walk into a prison instead of a bathroom. My father has walked into other realities as if they were other rooms, bouts of hallucination furnished by the patchwork images inconsistently flashing in his mind.

As the days passed, I tried my hand at domesticating the space. The bed was horribly uncomfortable, the quilt as itchy as horsehair, so I replaced it with an old duvet. Next, I dug out the blue vase from one of the boxes and filled it with flowers. My husband had always chided me about my penchant for buying bouquets. I'd bring them home, ignoring entirely my pollen sensitivity, and then I'd neglect changing their water, letting the vase and stems go over to a thin green muck like a filthy aquarium; finally, I'd forget all about them, until they began to stink, and I'd throw out some old food or clean the fridge before realizing it was the rotting flowers. I'd throw them out and the next day start the whole process over. Really I knew I shouldn't waste my time bringing flowers into the cell, but I thought it'd be nice to have a bit of color countering all the concrete. I placed them on the table. Some designers and decorators say a touch of paint, a couple of accent pieces, an objet here and there—you can really fix up a room with little effort. Unfortunately, my flowers, being so discordant with the rest of the space, only accented its bleak and fatal austerity. Still I brought in more flowers, I brought in scented candles, I brought in a couple of throw pillows and a nice blanket someone had knitted for me years ago and my slippers, convincing myself that one more thing would do it. It was the lighting, I thought. I couldn't turn off the overhead light, but I ran an extension cable from my bedroom and plugged in a friendly, fat little lamp that at least changed the sterile white light of the cell. I plugged in an electric kettle as well, then lined up my mugs on one of the storage bins. I even found a decorative bowl for my tea bags. That gave me the idea for some shelves, so I turned a few of the empty boxes on their sides and stacked them up behind the partition. Then I tucked the spare dining chair next to them and organized a few effects into a cozy reading nook. Though I dusted my hands together at a job well done and nodded to myself like it was all better now, in fact the sum of my efforts had been merely to create in the room a horrific dichotomy. A prisoner's cot was still the central object in the cell, and the cold and cruel facilities, rather than being stripped of their threats, instead tarnished all these plush domestic furnishings by proximity. It was grotesque and yet I found myself taking the kettle to the tap, pretending nothing was wrong (to who else but myself?), boiling water, and trying to snuggle up with a cup of tea on a cot mattress no more than two fingers thick.

I had hoped the guard would come back, maybe with an interest in conversation. I wanted to apologize to him. I hadn't meant to stir up anything, and I wasn't so naive to think that he wouldn't catch the blame if word of my circumstances began to circulate. He seemed in his own way nice enough. There are stories from prisons that make you think the guards are more criminal than the inmates. It's true enough about many of them, I suppose. I've seen headlines and photographs. "These types all end up as riot police in this country," I once told a friend I was trying to console after the arrest of her husband.

The second time we took my father to the hospital, a couple of years had passed. In the interim, a string of arrests struck Erdoğan's AK Party—pro-government bankers and businessmen, children of party leaders and high-profile politicians had been implicated in a gold-smuggling ring. The crackdown was driven by the Gülenists who dominated the judiciary branch of the government—followers of Fethullah Gülen, a former ally of Erdoğan and the AKP. Gülen and his faction had helped the AKP rise to prominence, until the Gezi Park protests and Erdoğan's subsequent increase in executive powers saw them eclipsed. The pro-government newspapers attacked the arrests as an attempted coup by a shadowy parallel state. The pro-Gülenist papers accused the government of plundering the people wholesale for their own benefit. For the leftists in the country, there was a sort of grotesque pleasure in watching these two factions try to eat each other, especially for my father and even, I admit, for myself. I wasn't particularly political but even I couldn't miss the government's slide into authoritarianism, the rampant police brutality, the trampling of human rights, the insidious infiltration of religious nationalism. It was easy, on the sidelines, to encourage these two factions to grapple in a gruesome battle to the death, forgetting entirely that the country was at stake. My father called me up every night that winter, shouting. He could be a loud man, charismatic. It could surprise you if you'd only seen him in his lecture halls or at his writing desk, where he was demure, studious, weighing his language. His diffidence came from a devotion to words that required he speak as precisely as possible. On family outings, however, particularly to places with an implied requirement of civilized decorum, or else while reading the paper at the breakfast table in his underwear, or else listening to the radio in the car as he dropped me off at school, and especially when we snuck a little rakı into him, he jettisoned any concern for the specificity of language and instead became a man who believed in passion as the only virtue, a devotee of fiery ecstasy. A quick tease against my father was another way to send him into a bout of shouting, though never, it must be said, at anyone.

He called me up every night that winter to make sure I was shouting about the government with him, that I was sharing in his crawling frustration. And I suppose I was. At the hospital, more and more mothers of the children I worked with wore headscarves. More and more of the kids were coming accompanied by fathers and grandfathers acting as interlocutors, translators of their injuries. Friends in the trauma center said the number of women coming in with stab wounds was climbing too, so many women covered in bruises so heavy they weighed down their bodies. Well, I started shouting with my father, saying I hoped these Gülenist judges would clear out all the rot. "No, no," Dad yelled. "They are rot and ruin too, they are just as bad, bad, bad." Then an hour later he'd call me up again, and I figured there was some new development, but instead he began repeating himself.

"I know, Dad. You said that."

"Right," he said, followed by an embarrassed pause. "Yeah. Right. Well, did you see what the foreign minister said today?"

"You told me."

"There's a lot to keep track of. You need to keep track,"

he said. "All this commotion, calamity here, calamity there—it's distracting."

Eventually the AKP weathered the corruption scandal. They instigated a witch hunt to purge the Gülenists, and hundreds of police investigators, lawyers, judges, and journalists were arrested. Dad called me up every night and we spoke for hours. It was nice.

Not long after, Aleppo fell to ISIL and the Syrian war started spilling into Turkey. Refugees in their millions were interred in sprawling tent cities near the border while the rest of Europe—worried now about the threat to their own countries—accepted a few thousand asylum seekers each and paid Turkey through the nose to keep the Syrians on this side of the Balkans. Then in 2015, a wave of bombings and shootings swept through the country: at the Istanbul Justice Palace, at the Bayrampaşa metro station, at the airport, near the Ayasofya, in Ankara, in Siirt, in Suruç, in Diyarbakır, and on into 2016, two in Ankara, seven in Istanbul, three in Diyarbakır, two in Gaziantep, in Dürümlü, Kayseri, Midyat, Lice, Şemdinli, Bursa— every other month a new disaster. ISIL was responsible for some of them, others were claimed by the PKK or blamed on them, and others still, the less investigated ones, were against Kurds: a wedding in Gaziantep, a rally in Diyarbakır. I saw photos on Facebook of the airport shootings, figures in the clumsy contortions of violence, no longer people but bodies, bodies uncensored and unblurred with their entrails on the sidewalk, pooling at the gutter where I had picked up and dropped off how many friends and relatives over the years? Three, four, five, six photos of the front doors of Atatürk Airport, where I had said hello and goodbye countless times—murder, murder under the bright sun like any other day.

Police raids followed the bombings, and swift press conferences with startlingly precise information about the number of the wounded and the dead, though my father told me over the phone that they did that to add credibility to the rest of whatever they said. "Just watch. The Turkish government never deals in approximations, because that is the space into which the opposition insinuates itself." Crackdowns and curfews were put into effect. In the east, elected Kurdish mayors were dismissed or arrested and replaced with governor-appointed ones. Leftist protests in the cities all ended the same: after a few hours, the police came in with their tanks and their tear gas and their night-sticks. Ultranationalist protests and rallies were allowed to tip briefly into violence, burning a few Arab shops or beating a few Kurds into pulp, before these nascent pogroms too were dispersed by riot police.

It was smack in the middle of all of this that my father had been attacked. Coming home from one of his classes at Boğaziçi University, he was followed by a stranger from the campus grounds, gone over to late spring verdure, down the switchback paths to the shore where my father sometimes strolled on his way back to the ferry landing. At an acute bend in the path, the man took out a gun and called out my father's name. My father turned, thinking it was a student or colleague catching up with him to suggest a cup of coffee along the waterfront. The man pulled the trigger but the gun hadn't been chambered, so in a few

74

bounds he closed the distance and tackled my father, using the butt of the gun as a club, breaking my father's nose and arm before the two were pulled apart by a passing group of students on their way to class.

The assailant was a political fanatic who had mistaken him for some grave threat to the nation. In fact, my father was mostly an academic who had made a name for himself beyond lecture halls as a minor novelist of inspired if inconsistent ability whose greatest talent was antagonizing the government. A few politicians condemned the attack but said it was my father who was in the wrong. They called him moronic to think such an attack wouldn't occur, to think that he could denigrate the Republic day in and day out for years with his trivial papers and thinly veiled satires he called novels and not get what he deserves.

The ER doctor said he'd need months of physical therapy. "We're brittle as we age, less elastic. Children are elastic. A newborn is exactly like an uninflated balloon. There is no difference." He would need a caretaker, a PT who could make house calls until he could himself travel to the therapist's office. "I have every confidence your father can make a full recovery. Still, it was a serious blow to the head he received."

Once again, he handed us over to a specialist who booked scans and tests, and took us to a little room where a different doctor now informed me my father's brain was shrinking. It was like a peeled orange, he said, and eventually, as all exposed oranges do, it will wither. My father had Alzheimer's. For a while still things might be quite normal, but he would have problems forming new memories. The doctor said that his tussle hadn't helped his condition. "In fact, if I may take an educated guess, maybe even it was detrimental." Eventually he would start losing his old memories as well. "Though it doesn't always happen chronologically," said the doctor.

He and the technician both said we were lucky my father was attacked; it gave them a reason to scan his brain and find he had Alzheimer's. There's no cure, though, so I wasn't sure if it was lucky to *find* it, but I knew what they meant. Finding it early just means life is perceived to last longer after discovery. It could be two years, it could be ten (almost never that long, though).

I was careful with the wheelchair as I guided him back to the car park, as if any little bump or knock would agitate his Alzheimer's. Foolish, foolish the way we become oversensitive to illness. Gingerly, after barking at him not to move his legs, I lifted one foot up and into the car, and then the other, and shuffled him back into the seat, and buckled him in. I told him that until we had proper instructions from the physical therapist about what movements and exercises he could perform, and in what manner, he'd better take it easy. "Even with therapy you'll have to get used to being wheeled around sometimes," I said. "We'll have to be careful about what foods you eat now, and what you drink—it's awfully important to stay hydrated." I don't know why I said any of this. It felt like I might say whatever popped into my head. I was talking as a way to keep other thoughts from cropping up, so I didn't have to think them and then speak them into the cramped space of my car.

On our drive back to my flat, my father asked to take the road far from the shore, through the hills. He told me to turn off the radio and crack the windows just a little and he closed his eyes. "Better not to be making memories right now anyway," he said.

Inexplicably, we stayed on in Turkey. Of course the guilt about keeping my father in a country that didn't want him anymore had begun to sink through my skin—but leaving always looks easier from the outside. How much do we bellyache when the nearest supermarket is closed and the next one is a half hour out of our way? How impossible then to cross a border—illusory or otherwise. I was unwilling to believe in freighted circumstances. I was ever an optimist.

My father relocated much of his life back into our flat in Ortaköy while he recovered from his injuries. We told ourselves it was temporary. The day he arrived, my husband spent all morning shuttling back and forth from Üsküdar with carloads of his things. While they were out, I noticed the blue vase my mother bought in İznik on the hallway table. In the dining room, I knew, there was another one. My mind swept across the flat, all the things that we'd had since my mom was alive. Bringing him back into this apartment would break his heart. Quickly I got to work, shutting knickknacks into cupboards, rolling rugs up and chucking them into the stairwell, peeling pictures out of their frames. I thought of it like a reluctant executioner thinks of their chore. In a whirlwind, I sterilized the house of its memories, still working as I heard my husband and father pull up downstairs, rushing, rushing as they buzzed into the building and rode the elevator up, greeting them breathlessly. My father was stoic as ever, unimpressed with his own misery. "We'll go for lots of walks," I told him. "We'll get out of the house as often as possible," as if there was something attached to his illness about being here, as if the flat was the site of his death. "We'll air it out too," I said. It was difficult watching him go to the chair by the window, his face inscrutable. I did not know if he was hurt more by the familiarity of the flat or by how much I had changed it. What do people injured by the past want? Relics and monuments of their pain? Some erasing wave of amnesia? Both impossibly at once?

My father was still, for the most part, his old self, which was a great comfort. The doctors had made it all sound rather bleak, yet here he was getting through his days without much trouble. His physical therapy progressed, and probably because he had all his life swum regularly, he was soon up and about again, going to cafés and to the university unaccompanied. This recovery lulled us all into a belief that he was truly getting better. There still seemed to be an endless allotment of time for him. Though he might forget something, it was nothing really shocking like what month it was or who we were or that he was hungry. Most of the time, after he paused to search for a word, he found it. He joked and called it his loading time. I took a picture of his face (slightly perturbed and furrowed as he was thinking of the right word), made it the background of my phone and called it my loading screen. He thought it was funny, but the next morning the joke had worn off. His sense of humor—something that, if you knew him only as a professor in that stiff pose at his desk while working on some somber bit of writing, you'd think he had very little of—was actually quite remarkable. More than anything else, he enjoyed laughing at himself, especially at aspects of himself no one else was comfortable teasing him for. He was remarkably adept at that black humor of self-deprecation, but this now was going away.

Occasionally a bank of fog would sweep over him and he would flounder through himself, flounder in whatever he was doing at the moment, but only for a moment. He had grown more impatient too, a little fickler if things weren't exactly how he'd wanted them, though doesn't this temperament strike us all as we age, as our bodies become vessels of pains and arthritis? Later I was filled with so much regret, thinking back on it, because these were the times of dignity, or posterity, or legacy, or whatever you want to call the vestigial moments of a life. I could have talked to him and made meaning of things with him.

No, he was beginning to live in a constant state of irritation—a toddler in need of a nap. It first struck me, I think, when we were in the waiting room of his physical therapist, flipping through magazines in an effort to ignore the television in the corner. One of the state-affiliated news stations was hosting a debate. We couldn't really hear them, but they kept showing the AKP flag, that ridiculous yellow light bulb on a white field.

"One light bulb to show they only ever had one idea in their heads," my dad whispered to me. "It's brighter too than all the party members."

"I don't know," said an old lady in the room, eavesdropping on us. "They make a lot of sense to me. There's more decency in Turkey now." She was wearing one of those fashionable tan trench coats made all the more popular by the president's wife, the sort that look like silk and have a seamless transition to the full headscarf. My father was the sort of secular Turk who considered the headscarf ban central to modern Turkish identity. He loathed its revival in the public sphere almost more than he loathed the people demanding women cover themselves. I admit I hated it too, hated how easy it was to fall into a misogynistic dichotomy of headscarf or anti-headscarf, how easy it was to politicize hair regardless of what you believed and how absolutely impossible it was to be a woman and exist without its politics, but I hated most of all how many women were never given a true choice in this country.

"Decency!" my father said. I apologized to the receptionist, but it wasn't long before my dad shouted: "Decency, decency!" again and then began hounding the woman, asking if she thought all those dead Kurds found solace in their murders because they paved the way to decency, if she thought all those child brides were glad to be sold off to decent men, if she thought students with their heads caved in by tear gas canisters were content in death because the state had acted *decently*. The receptionist stood up and started tutting at me, but my dad went on with his tirade.

"Shame on you," the old woman shouted back. She reached for her purse, an Hermès bag, and I saw a Chopard watch peek out from under her sleeve. She was the spitting image of the First Lady, the way some football fanatics watch the game in a full kit, shin guards and all, in worship of their heroes. "Shame on you!"

I helped my dad out of his chair and led him to the door before he could embroil himself in a full screaming match.

"Shame!" said the old lady. The receptionist was now coming between us as if prepared for some sort of geriatric fisticuffs to break out. "Shame!"

"Yes, yes, shame," I said, and told the old lady to go fuck herself.

I missed my husband, for all his panic. His nerves made me feel alive. Or I suppose, more accurately, my life had more in it because of his nerves—more chores, more head-aches, more responsibilities. We hadn't started in such a lopsided love, with him collapsing over every little crisis and me running around putting out the fires, but it wasn't his fault any more than it was mine. Life becomes a silt around your relationships, and before you know it, you're half buried and unable to adjust. And yet, as if the earth piled over us were nothing, my husband had flown off, leaving me alone in the crater of our marriage. Now waking up each morning did not feel like stepping out of a dream but instead slipping back under it. Coming home from the shops, or an errand at the pharmacy, did not feel like coming home, with all its unburdening. Every breath in the flat was swallowed with great difficulty, choking them prickly down. Often I would get home and walk straight through the flat to my bedroom and into the cell. The air in the prison was starkly different compared to my bedroom, the rest of the flat, all of Italy. It was a Turkish air, made up of the fine dusts and odors that come in the winds off the Marmara and Black Seas, off the steppes and mountains of Anatolia. When I breathed that air, it seemed like someone might walk by the door at any moment with a bit of simit still in their pocket, the sesame scent wafting through to me. The idea resuscitated me— even though truthfully it smelled only stale and clean in the cell, like the smell of loss, and reminded me not at all of my Istanbul. I can't explain how this imprisonment is not just another word for death.

But at times the air shifted more dramatically, and the cell was glutted in sunshine, though there were no windows, or filled with a concerto of street sounds: clay tavla discs slapping wooden boards, the tootling of small car horns, the winsome peals of white gulls in their gyres— like entering a hallucination, like taking a heady sip of ether, and I would sit there in those little puddles of happiness for hours.

After his attack, a friend of my father's, a fellow professor at the university named Berk, started coming to visit him. He still had not been allowed to return to work, and I could tell he missed not only his independence but his lecture hall as well. Berk was here to act as some sort of overseer of my father's health, his academic health that is. He'd pretend he was popping in but had called ahead each time to schedule it as if I imposed visiting hours.

Berk was about my father's age. The two of them had grown up, if not actually together, with the backdrop of the same experiences in the same city. The two of them talked a lot about the Cold War, the policies of the state during the sixties, seventies, and eighties; they talked a lot about the Soviet Union and the United States and the way journalism operated in those empires to help facilitate organized forgetting, and how the Turkish state emulated and improved upon these systems—especially after the 1980 coup. Back then, the new Press Law ushered in a wave of censorship against such words as *solidarity*, *equality*, and over two hundred others deemed too radical and threatening for national security, and so scrubbed them from television, newspapers, periodicals, books. This was the era in which my father and Berk had cut their teeth, and there were natural analogies with the current state of affairs in Turkey. But they thought governments still censored in the same way, still organized themselves around controlling a trickle of information and brutalizing lexicons. They did not understand how the world had changed, with a camera in every pocket, the global population one text message away. Even in Russia, where the regime maintained, through great effort, a level of control over thought, expression, information, gone were the days when you could transform Trotsky into a bit of concrete wall and river. Gone were the days when you could simply remove the word *anarchist* from the dictionary, and thereby excise anarchy from the state. It was the era of insurmountable information, where the problem was not insufficient language but far too much of it. Only the loudest are heard, and what is the fate of facts, then? What is the fate of reality when all manner of counterfeit narratives sweep over the people in ridiculous noise? What happens to the truth of things when those who whisper it can't be heard over the most grotesquely repeatable, the most engagingly idiotic, absurd, and outrageous lies? I didn't bother saying any of this to them.

During one of these visits, I cleared away their sandwich plates, brushing a few flakes of toast from my father's shirt and then doing the same for Berk, who reacted as if being tickled. They pulled out their cigarettes and I knew they would be settling in for a long and gray session of self-pity.

"He is a child," said Berk with a self-satisfied grin. "A playground bully who invites other idiots into his hierarchy of bullying."

I picked up their tea glasses and put an ashtray down between them. I didn't know if I'd call Erdoğan a bully; it seemed too tied up in psychoanalysis. It cheapened him as a threat to say he was just a malignant child.

"Would you want a child in charge of the country?" my father asked.

Berk had anticipated this. "What I mean is, obviously, that he is infantile in his mental capacities, and so infantile in his ability to inflict suffering."

"Don't you remember your own childhood?" I asked. "You'd beat another kid to death if they had a stutter."

I didn't think these visits were particularly good for my father (or Berk for that matter). From what I overheard, they were choked with melancholy and a residue of contempt. Yet my father sparred easily with his friend, capably rebutting points, his eyes flashing with an excitement that stood in even greater relief next to his purply bruised face, so perhaps it wasn't all bad that Berk paid frequent visits, even though the man insisted on bringing dour updates tucked into the pockets of his ratty blazer. My father's attack initiated a strange process of suspensions for professors, Berk included. Many were on probation pending an academic council's investigation. The government had insisted: an inquiry was necessary. Just because one was the victim of a crime didn't mean they themselves were incapable of criminal wrongdoing. A few of the professors had protested the inquiry and voiced concerns about the prosecutor's office taking an attack so lightly. Suddenly the group of them found themselves having to answer for phone calls to Germany, conferences in Sweden, papers published with co-authors in Israel.

He had handsome eyes. In fact, in the photos from his youth, I was convinced my father was quite handsome, much more so than my mother, whom I resented for giving me my looks. And even with so much of him gone now, he still had handsome eyes, or else the sort of eyes that gave the impression he was clever, very clever, perhaps ready to play a trick of some kind. They gave the impression that he understood what I was saying, and that he wanted to say something back, something more than *Yes, that's right*, but he couldn't overcome this obstacle in the mind.

At first, he had simply used synonyms. My father had an impossibly large vocabulary that came from years of reading and thinking about reading and taking great pride in the practice of circling words he did not know, looking them up, and using them ten times a day for a month. As a child, I thought that he was the man who invented the language, as no one ever said a word I had not heard my father say first. He was the administrator of words, appointed by the government. As I grew, I altered my theory slightly, imagining my father was instead the author of the dictionary. It was one of those brief yet indelible images that stayed with me well into adulthood so that, any time he mentioned the book he was writing, I always pictured the dictionary, and in this mental image he was not wearing his blazer and trousers but for some reason was dressed as a British barrister, sitting at his desk, writing his dictionary. My father, the lawyer of language, its keeper.

For a couple of years after the diagnosis, he could supplement a synonym for any word he was missing quite quickly, or else come up with some sort of amalgam image that was close enough, saying something like "long horse" when he meant giraffe. Over time the synonyms too started drying up, the words spreading out ever further from his grasp, retreating into the thin corners of his mind going over slowly to dementia. He became surprised at himself, surprised by his apparent stupidity, the chasm between all the things he knew he knew and all the things he could say. "Ah, Ayşe, I am losing my mind," he said, calling me my mother's name.

"I'm not Ayşe," I would say.

"Yes, you don't have to remind me. I know, but I can't seem to say anything else. What is the word?" This became his most common question whenever we spoke, whenever I tried taking him out of the house and down to the greengrocer or café or bookshop to get a little exercise. He would begin to tell me something, trying to put on a memory the way you might try on shoes at the mall, but he would get to a point, a word that was obvious given the context (*boat*, *turtle*, *photograph*, *ice cream*), and he would stop, laugh at himself, say he was much more stupid than a professor ought to be, and ask me what is the word. If I gave it to him, he would laugh again, and try to remember what he was saying. If I withheld it, in part to help him practice, in part overcome by a wave of petty cruelty, he would stop in silence for a long time, thinking, thinking, and I could see the industry of his thought, I could read the effort in those handsome eyes, but in the end, he came up with nothing except a hollow giggle, and then he would say: "This is not correct." His refrain, now; the sentence that will be the last remaining to him.

PART III

WE WENT TO THE optometrist just north of the Convento Trinita, with its wide park and surprisingly ornate fountain. The jets were off for the winter, and the fruit trees scattered about the grounds shivered in their dormant dreams. The optometrist was a generous woman, one of the only locals who didn't seem to care about my poor Italian, and never made some facetious comment about my accent either (you know the type—*darling, you're doing so well; darling, it's enough you escaped that awful country*). Every time I came by, she measured my vision, recommended a few frames that were usually the most flattering rather than the most expensive, and sent me on my happy way. Today should've been just the same, but I had to bring my father along. People find it entertaining when parents take their children on leashes to amusement parks and hiking trails, but they probably draw the line at doing that to the elderly; I would have the police sent after me for abuse if I dragged my father around in a harness.

When we arrived, I asked the nurse at the front desk

if they had any magazines. She gave me the one she was reading, and I handed it to my father and told him to stay calm and sit still in this comfy chair and wait for me. The nurse smiled at me and smiled at my father, and the optometrist came out and I handed her my glasses. I'd snapped one arm and cracked a lens last night. After putting my father to bed, I'd gone to the kitchen to make some tea and in the half darkness I did not see my glasses on the counter (I never left them on the counter—I suspected my father mistook them for his own and left them there) and set a stack of pots on them while rooting around for my çaydanlık.

The optometrist pursed her lips. "No, I can't fix that. How old is the prescription, anyway?"

I shrugged.

She asked if I wanted to get my eyes tested as well, or just pick out replacement frames for the old prescription. I asked if it would cost me anything to have my eyes tested.

"Free if you buy frames."

She took me back to a small room, too small really for all the testing equipment. It was a fast few minutes and I was released to the front of the shop, where I saw the nurse smile at me but my father was missing from the scene.

"Oh, the man," I said to the receptionist-nurse, pointing at the empty chair in the waiting corner.

"The man," she said, and came out from behind her desk, did a quick spin, and went out the door to check the street.

The front of the shop was a maze of tightly packed

display cases, hundreds of model frames folded and resting on walls full of little nose stubs, and turning one corner and then a second, I found my father at a dead end.
Embarrassed, I called out to the nurse and the optometrist
(who'd gone out to help the search). I apologized out of
one corner of my mouth while chastising my father like
an errant toddler out of the other. Then I asked which
frames were in the basic range, and the receptionist-nurse
steered me to a case near the door. I tried a pair on and
put it back and tried another pair on and put it back;
meanwhile my father, standing beside me, started mimicking my motions, putting a pair of glasses up to his face
though he already had his own on, and putting them back.
I found a set I liked and went to the counter, tripping on
my father's cane, which he had left immediately behind me
and so perfectly out of my field of vision you'd think he'd
planned it. My stumble and the clatter of the stick made
the receptionist-nurse jump. I told her I was ready. She
tried to sell me the ultra-strong, ultra-thin lenses, saying
I could back a bulldozer over them (do people often find
their glasses under bulldozers?). I paid and went back to
collect my father, but his glasses were gone. His arms were
moving strangely, like he couldn't figure out how to use
them. A half dozen pairs of frames were in a pile at his
feet. He pulled a pair of glasses off the case and held them
up to his face before dropping them to the floor.

"Dad, where are your glasses?"

"What's the matter?" asked the optometrist.

"Dad, look at me."

"What?" asked the optometrist.

He must've taken his own glasses off and set them in the case amid all the dummy pairs.

"What color are yours?" I asked, unable to picture them.

"Tell me, what language is that? Is everything alright?" asked the nurse-receptionist.

My father pulled another pair of glasses down and dropped them, pulled down another pair and dropped those too, over and over until the pile was up to his ankles; he'd cleared half a case.

"Hey, you can't—"

"Just a moment, please," I said. I started putting the frames back as he dropped them, bumping into him by accident, and as he stumbled to the side, I heard the squeak and crunch of frames under his shoes.

"This is not correct!"

The optometrist tried to be accommodating, but her nurse started squealing out, scolding me for mishandling the merchandise. "Think of the cost!" she said.

"This is not correct!" My father was going at it now, pulling down pair after pair in a frenzy, groping and swiping at the air until he managed to bump a case hard enough that it came tumbling down.

"What's the matter with you people!" cried the receptionist-nurse.

I tried righting the case, then swept an armful of frames up into the hem of my shirt. My father, struggling as he went, climbed down to the floor and grabbed frame after frame, smashing them in his hands as he went. "This is not correct! This is not correct! This is not correct! This is not correct!"

I was standing in the living room, watching my father doze in his chair, when I heard the hollow clang of a heavy door closing through the wall. I went to investigate, and from my cell, I heard more sounds coming from the corridor: the clopping of boots or heavy-soled shoes on the concrete floor, keys jangling on a ring. A prisoner perhaps, on their way to jail, a guest with whom I could chat, since it seemed the guard would go out of his way to ignore me in here. I tried peering through the bars, but they were too close together to see beyond a meter or two either side of my cell. I heard the guard's voice, though, coming down the hallway, then finally he came into view, walking with another man ten or twelve steps away.

"As I was saying . . ." the guard went on, switching now which side of the corridor he was walking on, to put himself between me and the man. He pointed at the opposite wall to distract the man as they approached me, but there wasn't anything to point at; it was just a wall. He started exaggerating the swing of his arms and turning his torso as if he were trying to completely block the man's view of the cells as they passed. This pantomime would've worked (though it wasn't necessary, since the other man was entirely focused on the clipboard he was carrying), had I not, just as they passed me, said: "Hello, good to see you again!"

Both men stopped in their tracks. The supervisor stared at me. "What's going on here?" he asked.

"What's going on?" the guard shouted, pretending, I guess, never to have seen me before. I half expected him to take a step back, out of sight of the other man, and mime slitting his throat while holding a finger to his lips.

"Would you like some tea?" I asked. "I've just made a pot."

The supervisor paused, considering the tea, but then shook his head and patted his large belly, showing he was full. "I've got too much to do today," he said.

"What is it you're doing?"

"Preparing, preparing. I'm in charge of all this, you see." He turned to leave. "But what are you doing here? What is she doing here?" He craned his neck to see all my cozy decorations and amenities. "Tea?"

I explained to the supervisor what had happened, how I'd gotten to be in his prison, where the door behind me led. He patiently listened as I asked if he might be able to help me out. "I mean, I'm not saying it is your fault, but you are the authority around here," I said. "I'd just like my bathroom put back." Even as I said it, I wasn't sure whether it was true.

The prison, it turned out, had been undergoing an extensive expansion, despite the total lack of space left in the penal campus grounds. "The construction crew must've been looking for space wherever they could. So you see . . ."

". . . see what?"

"Well . . . they must've found some in your closet."

"Bathroom."

"Yes."

"They're expanding the prison?" I asked.

"They are expanding the prison," said the supervisor.

"Expanding it!" shouted the guard.

"Why are they expanding it?" I asked. "There's no one in here."

"There will be plenty of people in here soon."

"There will be!"

"You have to have a prison before you can have prisoners," the supervisor continued. "You have to make room for criminals before you can have criminals."

"That's backward," I said.

"Backward!" cried the guard, stifling himself. "Excuse me."

"Well, they must put the space back!" I said.

"Come now, you can't expect a contemporary prison to conduct itself in an outdated manner. Criminals are a given in society. They are as unavoidable as . . . as . . . unavoidable. So a prison must be under a constant state of renovation and expansion. Inevitably, room begins to run out, of course, that is why there is more than one prison in the world, but there is something to be said for keeping the prisoners to one large complex, something to be said about the continuity of space. Who are you to question this?"

"I'm the one without a bathroom!"

"Yes. Keep quiet. Keep very quiet, I shouldn't like to think what might happen if we see or hear you again," the supervisor said, not so much threatening me himself as invoking the threat of some higher authority against both of us. "So the builders look for room wherever they can find it. Is that enough to fuss over? Life is full of little hindrances. Why just this morning . . ."

The supervisor and the guard had been slowly backing away from me throughout this speech. Eventually they turned and walked down the hall, the supervisor still talking, but addressing only the guard—gone.

It's midsummer and bombs are going off around us.

Sometimes history announces itself into our lives weeks in advance, and other times it arrives with no great introduction, giving you, quite impolitely, no chance to commit anything to memory. I can't remember anything at all about the day. As on many July days in my life, I must have complained about the humidity and spent the unbusy hours at work under the air conditioner. "You'll make yourself sick," one of the nurses always told me. Pneumonia, I think she meant, though she never said it. This always right after coming back from her cigarette break.

I'm not sure what we were doing that evening. Probably my father, unable to wait for me to get home and make dinner, had boiled up a packet of soup mix (the only thing he ever bought at the supermarket), and settled in for the night in his lounge chair. He was still living with us, though he'd long since regained his strength and, thanks to all the physical therapy, could walk without a cane and use the stairs and lift things over his head with even greater ease than before his attack. We kept him in our flat out of laziness, a complete lack of desire in any of us (my father included) to help him move yet again, pack and haul boxes, go to bureaucrats' offices and change his address on a million different registries. It was easier for him to get to work from Ortaköy, anyway, and he had been quite insistent on that point. He would return to his lectures at the university as soon as he was able. It made sense I guess for him to stay with us, but this uncertain state of residence had given rise to a few odd habits. Most guilt-inducing of all was that he still kept his toothbrush and deodorant in his suitcase in his room, as if we would not allow him to claim a small parcel of counter space in the bathroom.

That night, my husband would have been in our bedroom, or showering, or maybe was still on his way home. No, he couldn't have been coming home, he'd have died of fright if he had been caught in the streets that night, so I will say that I was in the kitchen making dinner for the three of us while my father was spoiling his appetite in the living room and my husband was washing his face. Something like an explosion cut open the sky. It might have been an earthquake, everything in the apartment briefly rattled, and standing at the stove I was thinking it a shame to have wasted such good cuts of beef right before the earth swallowed us up.

My husband shouted from the bedroom, and my father dropped his soup everywhere, but the earthquake hardly lasted a moment, the odds and ends of the house shivering once or twice in their places before everything went calm. I turned the stove down to simmer and went to take stock of any damage in the flat.

Meanwhile in the street below, people were in chaos, their worries painting up the whole neighborhood. Someone on a megaphone barked that there was a curfew, there was no need to step outside or even go near the windows, just go to bed, there's a curfew. My husband had jumped into bed and pulled the covers over his head. I went back to the kitchen, where my father was standing at the window. I stood beside him for a moment, then moved toward the balcony door, and he grabbed my arm but did not stop me. I put my hand over his and we hobbled together onto the balcony.

A large tank rolled by, the kind for transporting a mess of soldiers quickly. Out the top hatch was the man on the megaphone telling everyone to stay indoors; their lives depended on it. Half the neighborhood went down into the street, throwing complaints in his direction—about their rhododendrons being trampled by the tracks, or the racket the tanks were making on a weeknight, or about their unending feud with a neighbor over the vegetable garden (this particular idiot—you know the type—saw the commotion as the perfect opportunity to bring their domestic grievances to the attention of those with authority).

The tank came to a stop by the taxi stand up the street, and a dozen or so soldiers tumbled out its belly and took positions at corners and terraces and low walls, as if they were petulant children roused from a palace dream, and not men with black rifles in their hands. My father hollered something down to them but no one listened. The balcony railing trembled. Then screaming through the air, a jet fighter darted overhead, issuing a sonic boom throughout the neighborhood that threatened to send the balcony jumping right off the side of the building. My father and I ducked back inside to find that my husband had flipped the bed over and propped it against the wall as if bracing it against another explosion. Frantic, he piled up pillows in the windows to protect against shattering glass. Catching on, I went to grab the heavy couch cushions and stack them against the windows in the living room, as my father pulled blankets, duvets, towels, and tablecloths out of the linen closet, draping first himself and then each of us in turn with them.

Between stacking up cushions and blankets, we scrolled through our phones. Social media was abuzz with updates, corrections, speculations—alerts pinged by the minute. On TV, news outlets were saying it was a military takeover. Here onto the screen came two soldiers with guns pointed at the anchor, telling them to announce a successful coup had just occurred. "The administration of the country has been completely taken over in order to reinstate constitutional order," said the anchor. "A curfew is in effect, a new constitution will be prepared, the government of Tayyip Erdoğan has eroded democracy and will face justice." The station went out. My husband crawled out of our shelter to fetch his computer and mine. We had four or five screens in front of us, each of them collapsing echoes of the others in a kaleidoscope of chaos. Another heavy sound slid across the sky and slapped the air with a boom.

"Bombs!" my husband screamed. "Bombs! They're bombing us!" He screamed on and on as the tumult outside shattered through me in fissures of sound. The screech of tank tracks, the blare of the megaphone, the chants, the commands, the hundreds of shoes over the street, the stamp of a few dozen boots, the calls from the buildings, the far-off crack of gunshots, the low hum of helicopters invisible in the black sky, the barrel beat of hands against chests, the buzz, the buzz, the buzz—I was filled to the brim with noise until there was nothing else in me but all the clamor of the night march rolling into a terrible, edgeless dread.

The obvious things were the first to go: streaming services, the landline, my father's cell phone. But our sudden destitution, in the aftermath of my husband's departure, revealed the enormous redundancy in our possessions. My father had brought with him his own cookware set, his own plates and bowls and silverware, his own vacuum cleaner, his own kitchen table, his own suitcases, cocktail shaker, candelabras, rugs, stamps, toilet cleaner, ironing board, stepladder—didn't we get rid of anything when we moved him out of his flat? Didn't we throw out so much? And yet here were all these items stacked and piled around his bed, next to the wardrobe, on the nightstand, the windowsills—duplicates of things we already owned.

I tried selling what I could online, describing it as a new year sale, and over the course of a few days I was able to make a month's expenditure this way. My father watched me as I worked, blocking my path through the topiary maze of his room as a way to communicate something, or else pushing the top end of a rolled-up rug with a smile until it tipped over, to communicate something else. He watched as strangers arrived in the flat and absconded with the objects of his life. I was happy to have more air, more light, space for him to unfurl a bit, as if that would slow his decline.

Next, I turned down the heating and wrapped my father in his winter coat and two blankets, and did the same for myself. We huddled near each other on the couch but not near enough to warm one another. We weren't really this desperate, not yet, but the idea of turning off the heat knowing it could be turned back on gave me a sense of security, allowed us almost to practice. Austerity still felt a bit like a game, something novel and silly that feels almost satisfying when you manage to put up with it, last for a while through it, because you feel then that you really are prepared, you really can handle being deprived, you take pride in the monkish poverty you've just endured, and then you loosen up the purse strings for a little treat while you still can. I knew better than to feel this way. I was ashamed to find joy in our burgeoning hardship, to belittle the difficulties so many others in this world live as truth and can't escape. In any event, if we were frugal with the heat now, we might make it all the way to spring without having it shut off, and then it wouldn't matter. We could live without heating and electricity through the long, warm days of Italian summer, and read books free from the library and sell our winter clothes, and maybe make it through the summer, and maybe even beyond that, maybe long enough just to begin needing the sweaters and jackets again, needing the heating again—but that was a long way to go, anything could happen.

I had made a little game out of waiting for the other inmates to show up. Once or twice a day, usually after setting my father in front of the television for his morning programs, or after putting him down for a nap, I'd hop into the cell and watch through the door for a half hour or so, thinking very carefully that a new prisoner would show up in thirty seconds exactly, trying to will it. I'd keep my face turned slightly, looking at the table in the room or my own things so that the edge of my vision was on the door, and I'd count down, and around three or four I'd slow each pause to three, five seconds, ten seconds, twenty seconds, then snap my gaze back to the door, but there was nothing so I'd start counting down again. A fascination had bloomed under my thoughts. I was fixedly curious about these prisoners—where were they, all these criminals the supervisor had said were like a wave sweeping the country?

I wanted to ask them who they were, where they were from, what they did to end up here. Wasn't that the most important question for a prisoner? What are you in for?

Would we have enough time to cover everything as they trooped past my little window? What would I say in return? Would they bother asking me about myself? I didn't think I looked like a criminal, but they'd ask me, surely, and if I didn't prepare an answer, I might let something slip. Well, I wasn't that inept. Life wasn't a sitcom with lots of forehead slapping. It was only a few days later, as I was coming up with yet another backstory for myself (I had killed my stepbrother because he'd beaten his girlfriend), when they brought in the first prisoner.

The woman had a very wide nose, a nose that took up most of her face and overhung the thin lips of her mouth, flanked by large, pronounced cheekbones that gave her a strangely gaunt appearance. Yes, she looked pulled, as if a child had grabbed hold of the sides of her face and with enthusiastic affection stretched her wide. I thought she must have a large smile but I would not see it. I thought she didn't look like a criminal. Or rather, all of this occurred to me in the brief moment that it took for the guard to walk her by my cell. I didn't notice much else of her; in fact, she could have been completely without a body, her face was so striking I never would've noticed. In the shock of the long-awaited moment, I forgot to say anything at all. The sudden appearance of this woman seemed to crack the facade of the place. Yes, there was a prison guard and a prison supervisor, but a part of me was still holding on to the idea that my cell was a fantasy, a curiosity, that it was more than just a glum little room with an iron cot and a steel toilet. But of course, it wasn't, as the arrival of the first prisoner now made that fact unavoidable.

I waited as the guards locked her in her cell.

Cautiously I whispered a little—*psst!* I heard only the muted echo of myself jumping down the hallway. "Hey!" I whispered a little louder. "Can you hear me?" I didn't want to bring the guard running back, but I tried once more, speaking properly this time. "Are you there? Are you going to say something?" No one replied. She must be able to hear me. "Hey!" I shouted.

"Shut up," a woman's voice replied.

"Who are you?" I asked, this time at a normal volume.

"Zeynep," she said as if that meant something to me, but I guess I had been the one to ask the foolish question.

"Where are you from?"

"Quiet," she said. *Quiet.* The way she said it touched the bone of my wrist and traveled up my arm. It sounded familiar to me; her voice was crawling up out of the shadows of my memory, but I didn't know any Zeyneps.

"What did you do?"

She hushed me: "The police are everywhere!"

"Well of course, we're in a prison."

"Stop it!" She seemed to be moving around the cell; her voice paced nervously back and forth in the air, weaving like a grist of bees about their hive. "No more of this."

"You don't look like a criminal."

"I'm a journalist," she said.

I kept calling out to her, kept asking her questions. She didn't answer me.

For a long time, I thought I was a bad daughter because we didn't leave. In a few short years, my father had suffered a psychotic episode, been attacked, placed on leave from his professorship, diagnosed with Alzheimer's, permanently removed from his post, then blacklisted by every other university in the city. A good daughter would've forced her father out of the country that had tried to kill him. Meanwhile, once a week, my husband pleaded that we go on a vacation to Germany or France or England. "Look how nice Montenegro is," he said. "Look here at these cities in Croatia, they're just a cruise away."

"They're close to Italy," I said. I had only been to Italy once, a beach vacation at the end of high school to the coast of Liguria, but I had fallen in love quickly, as I like to do.

"Yes," said my husband, producing now seamlessly a map, as if people still kept atlases folded up in their pockets. On it he had a thick line in Sharpie drawn from Istanbul to Thessaloniki, and from there to Bar, Montenegro, then Bari, Italy, then Milan, Zürich, Frankfurt, Cologne, Amsterdam.

"Amsterdam?"

"The Hague. The International Courts are there," he said, as if those were enticing spots to spend leisurely summer days.

"Courthouses aren't like force fields," I told him.

"No, no. This is just one of many road trips I've planned. We could go to Denmark, or Sweden. The fjords."

There are many Turks in Sweden, political exiles most of them. The map he showed me was well used, with other lines of escape pencil-marked and erased. Maybe, maybe, I told him, shrugging my shoulders. He seemed to flicker for a moment like an unprotected candle flame.

As we inched cautiously through the winter of 2016 and into 2017, he forwarded me email after email from travel agencies. I told him I might need to renew my passport. "My god, Dilara, that is ridiculous. It can take months to get it renewed! How are we supposed to go to Croatia?"

"Croatia?"

"Or wherever." He said we needed a vacation, and I knew he meant one from which he had no intention of returning. He was terrified, perhaps selfishly, of staying— more afraid for himself than for my father. My husband had always been a nervous sort, yet this level of paranoia was new after the attempted coup, nearly laughable to me, but I should've been scared too. In truth, I had not ever considered leaving. Not once in all the mess that grew around us had I considered that we must escape, even when everything had exploded the previous summer.

Peripherally, I knew someone who had been killed in the coup attempt. There had been relatively few fatalities that night, despite the number of people out on the streets, despite the tanks, despite the jets and helicopters, despite all the soldiers with guns. She was a young woman who worked at the hospital on the cleaning staff, who had been shot one hundred meters from the Bosporus Bridge. Six other people in the street with her had also been shot dead. Everyone ran away except the soldiers who barricaded the bridge, barricaded both bridges and fired on anyone who approached them. Through the night helicopters and jets whizzed overhead. In Ankara, putschist and state aircraft shot each other out of the sky and fired rockets into the parliament building. In Istanbul the din of explosions continued well into the morning, rattling our walls and windows, the sound slightly muffled by our cocoon of mattresses and pillows and cushions. From inside our barricade, we watched footage of different groups of soldiers all standing around and pointing their guns at people over and over, the same few videos of streets drowned in floodlights and shouts and a few pops of rifle fire. We flipped between stations, the state-run TRT and Anadolu, and then CNN Türk. In the middle of the night, the news stations reported on the president's whereabouts, how he had been on holiday in the south and narrowly escaped a group of assassins sent after him. Erdoğan's fighter escorts were battling rebel jets on the way back to Istanbul. Then the news anchor's voice became very serious. The video feed cut back to the studio, and she took her lapel microphone off and said she had the president on the line right now. She showed her phone to the camera. The president had called via FaceTime from aboard his plane. She held her microphone up to her cell phone and asked what was going on, what should the people do?

"We will overcome this," he said. "Take to the streets. My people must take to the streets and give these criminals their answer. I am coming, I am coming and my people will meet me in the streets."

"What a prophet," my father said, almost crying. I couldn't understand his reaction at first. Or rather, I understood it, understood his anger, his plummeting disappointment in the people, always so easily duped in his eyes, but I couldn't feel anything myself. Everything was too surreal, incredibly far away and almost impossible to believe in. Even having seen a coup before, even living through these attacks, the events now flashing before my eyes seemed amorphous, two-dimensional as shadow theater. Erdoğan was calling into a news station while escaping pursuing fighter jets. The people outside our building had started crawling down to the streets to meet the blinding floodlights, the grave and somber soldiers. The muezzins, as if on command, as if it had taken them no time at all to travel to their mosques and climb their minarets, began chanting Erdoğan's words from their parapets: "Give these criminals our answer!"

The putschists closed the Istanbul airport, drove their tanks right onto the runways, hoping to catch Erdoğan there, but the people would not stay in their homes. The people came and pulled the soldiers down from their tanks and trucks and beat them to death. They cleared the airport and the president landed in Istanbul, landed on a runway full of people, so full it looked like the plane climbed down out of the sky into a sea of bodies.

"We will overcome this!" was the refrain, and it was echoed in the minarets by the muezzins, in the cars and cars of people now filling the streets and blaring their horns, in the newsrooms and on television, in the elevator outside our door, in the adjoining flats. All the sounds of the city battered against our windows, and inside the flat they were duplicated through our TV and laptops and cell phones. Inside our cave of cushions and carpets, all of our screens shone with duplicate images from duplicate angles, a soldier on a tank became five soldiers on five tanks, a dozen people throwing stones became a mob, a fire was all fires. Everything was happening over again, events on top of themselves, images of soldiers, of people, of rifles and tanks, of politicians, of explosions, it was all the same and different, and so grotesquely discordant with our little fort of pillows, our strange childhood construction, a soft cloister against the death ringing down the avenue.

At last, as dawn approached—one of those early summer dawns so laden with sun they flood the body with morning—the television showed soldiers in Taksim Square, surrounded now by loyalist police forces, piling their guns up and surrendering. The holdouts on the bridges too, some seven hundred soldiers, at last fell down from their tanks and threw up their arms and became the mercy of the people.

"He is immortal now," my father said. "There is no one else but Erdoğan."

"The coup is a gift from God," said Erdoğan in a speech that morning. It was the phrase that would come to encompass his policy for the next two years and the start of a state of emergency that opened the door for the swift removal of all political checks and protections for dissent. Once again Gülen was invoked as the enemy of the Republic, the puppet master of a deep state. Whether it was true or not I didn't care, and in practice it didn't matter; *Gülen* was simply a dog whistle meaning anyone critical of the regime, or with too many degrees, or who spoke Kurdish or Arabic, or was a communist, or was trans or homosexual or an unmarried woman, or childless: anyone who undermined the state by breathing, beating, living.

My father used to say they would arrest anyone. He had been arrested himself, after all, back in 1975 when he was a student caught up in the violence between right- and left-wing nationalist groups, but was let out a year later. He used to say they'd throw you in jail for a bad joke, and while that was true, it had happened before, it had always felt hyperbolic somehow. The level of state surveillance in his youth wasn't as pervasive. After the coup attempt, however, they really were arresting everyone. We knew plenty of people who might never again be free. The police were everywhere. You had to credit them. They weren't an infinite number, they weren't even a one-to-one ratio with the citizenry, but it felt like they were. The paranoid thought crept in that there must be at least five, maybe ten police for each civilian. They arrested people day and night. You would think that eventually the country would run out of citizens to arrest. I did wonder at times how many of these unlucky strangers might be actors, only pretending to be arrested, in this country full of conspiracy and the threat of sabotage. It would keep up morale, or rather keep us inundated. I watched clips of them, scanning for repeated moles or distinctive hairlines or ridges of the nose, facial features I had seen before under different wigs. In a way it didn't matter if people were arrested or not, only that everyone believed they were being arrested. But maybe the country was bigger than I realized, big enough to supply the bodies for all these arrests with no need for subterfuge. Imagining a hundred people is easy enough, but a million individual people, a million of anything, what does that look like, really? Tens of millions? There are only thirty-some teeth and that feels like a lot.

My father's name appeared on a list of over six hundred professors throughout Turkey who were now purged from their positions by presidential decree. A few weeks later, I was fired from my position in the hospital. It was a precaution, my supervisor said, because of my ties to the dissident author, my father. Catching wind of the trouble, the third-party agency that had arranged my contract at the hospital called to announce that they were expunging my account from their database. By the end of the month, the elementary school had sacked me too. They would find someone else to test their pupils for learning disabilities.

I couldn't find another school to hire me. I contacted the few other agencies in Istanbul but none returned my calls. My aunts and uncle had to be careful about calling and texting us, arriving unannounced to spare some record of our relation, and visiting later and later at night, as if the sun were an agent of the regime. By some miracle my husband kept his job, though he had been due for a promotion that summer and instead saw his salary slashed. He came home each evening with a fresh pack of cigarettes, having smoked a whole pack at work.

"You need to take care of yourself," I told him.

"Stop, stop," he said. When I took his hands, they jumped like frogs out of my palms. Always now, when I touched him—his shoulder, his arm, his hands, the temple of his head—that part of his body leapt away for an instant before drawing back in a circle like a cautious dog, or, perhaps more accurately, like shell shock. I put his fingers to my lips and pressed them hard together, pushing, pushing my lips against his shivering skin and feeling the ruins of my husband.

My father told me a lot that he was sorry for everything his life had done to my life. "It is meaningless for me to say this, though. It is the apology owed all children by their parents."

Like a coin jumping into a fountain, my husband called me up and said that he was sorry.

"Right."

"I left too fast; I didn't pack enough sweaters," he said.

"It's cold here, too."

"Is the radiator valve stuck?" he asked me.

"Could be," I said. I didn't want to tell him that I'd turned it off.

"It sticks every year. You'll need a wrench."

I laughed. It wasn't much of a laugh, one of those little sniffs. It was stupid to talk like this but I didn't want to say anything else. I wanted to carry on, like my husband might be ringing from the garage, just an hour or two before coming home from work—checking in and asking if he should get a loaf of bread on the way. Then he said more sharply: "Dilara, it's unnatural!" and I knew that he meant the prison and that we would have to talk about it after all. "Don't you think you ought to call the authorities? The Italians, I mean."

I kept laughing at him. I missed his rattling anxiety, the electricity of it, the way it made life feel quite exciting.

"You're not safe," he said into the receiver.

"Yes."

"Why are you laughing at this?"

"I'm not. I am laughing because of you."

"Are you mad at me?"

I sighed as hard as I could, I sighed so that the phone would rattle in his hand, would make him jump out of his shoes and up into the sky, would send him flying home in an instant.

"You left your anxiety medication," I said. It was still on the kitchen counter, in a little dish because he hated pulling the pills out of the prescription bottle. I held them over the sink, about to pour them down the drain.

"It's alright," he said. "I've already gone through withdrawal."

I set the dish back in its place, thinking about the risk that my father might mistake them for some of his own pills, and leaving them there.

"Are you remembering to lock the door?" my husband asked. Throughout our marriage, wherever we had lived, I never thought about locking up at night. Usually, he did it on his way to bed. He'd installed extra locks on our flat in Ortaköy when a neighbor mentioned their bike was stolen. But some nights, when I stayed up much later than him, he'd left them for me to lock, and I'd forget, and we'd wake to find the house exactly as we left it, locks unbolted, and he'd pout all day about how I didn't mind whether we were robbed, whether he was killed by roving thieves in the night. When he was like this, I took pleasure in that affectionate kind of ridicule between spouses. I called him Mr. Melodramatic and he, because he was in love with me, after all, responded by becoming extra melodramatic, teasing my teasing in return.

I had expected that exile should change him, that a frivolous country would make him frivolous, and at first it seemed like it had. At a restaurant one night, maybe three or four months after we had come to Italy, he started shouting that I didn't understand myself. "Don't you get what the curve of your ears is, that bit of your hair that tucks over it? Don't you understand the long line of your nose? You mustn't or you would be like me, stupefied! The quick light of your eyes, and yet you are not intoxicated by your own magic!" I laughed then, as I so often laughed at him. The Italians in the restaurant thought who-knows-what about this agitated man shouting in a foreign language. His skittish energy had produced these outbursts before—grand proclamations of epiphany or love—and in fact this was a tendency he shared with most of my family members. We were demonstrative, we liked to shout out our beliefs. But as the weeks went by, and he went on shouting, I realized his rants were less and less about the president, the regime, my father, his gnawing and overactive though not entirely meritless fear of being arrested, tortured, executed. He shouted instead these silly declarations, practicing his Italian at the same time, basking casually on a sunny beach with a cool and scented drink in his hand: "The sea is marvelous! The woman is marvelous! The day is marvelous!" and he stole many swift kisses from my cheek between his outbursts.

I should have known better than to think he would change for good. His anxiety, briefly dormant, quickly found new outlets: swapping fear of the state for fears about his health, fears of the economy and our bank accounts, fears of black mold, and fears of foundation issues in the building. He was particularly paranoid about the neighbors. It didn't help that they leered at us, mistaking us for Arabs (with whom, many of them told me, they certainly sympathized, but they begged them to seek refuge in richer countries) and distrusting our mother tongue. So over time my husband became graver, treating the small happenings of life even more seriously than before. We lived in a quiet enough town, but it had its coarse edges, stolen mopeds, broken car windows, TVs whisked away in the night. He scolded me when I left the doors unlocked. I think he saw in me sometimes a burden. How strange to miss someone's unkindness.

"No, no. I leave the house open every night. The doors are wide open, Mr. Melodramatic. You'll have to come and lock them."

He didn't take the bait. "What if something were to happen to your father?"

"A killer on the prowl, eh?"

"Or just a kid with a knife," he said.

"Who knows, maybe even a wandering nurse who serially cares for the sick."

"Don't joke," he said. This time it was him sighing, and the soft sound tore through me.

I asked him where he was calling from and he said he had made it to Milan and was staying in a ramshackle hostel on the north edge of town. He hadn't decided if he would stay there or go on to Turin, or even cross the Alps to Switzerland. That was how he said it. "Maybe I will try to cross over the Alps. To Switzerland."

"You're not running from the Nazis."

"That is a matter of semantics," he said.

"You could head south for the winter," I said.

"Please leave the flat. Please come to Milan."

"They might be listening to this call. Now they know where you are." This was cruel, more torturing than teasing, but he left me here in this village outside Salerno. He left me alone with my hunched father, and the hunched-shoulder mountains of the Apennines.

"Do you need any money?" he asked.

I did, of course. I didn't say that. Not because I wanted to seem strong, as if I didn't need him and had gotten along just fine in the wake of his abandonment—we didn't have that kind of relationship, more rivals than partners. It was because I knew he needed money too, and he didn't have a job, and I thought of him lying in bed each night, swallowing and swallowing down the knot of fear in his throat, nearly choking on it.

"Do you really think they're watching you?" I didn't like using this vague *they* for the government. I meant the state, my state, the regime, the president, his party, the parliament ministers that worked every day at destroying the humanity of their fellow ministers, but in conversation with my husband, even with my father, it was always *they*.

"They're watching you," he said.

"Wouldn't the last place they'd expect to find you be here at home with us?"

"Please," he said. "You must leave."

Soon after we arrived in Italy, I suggested looking into other Turks in the area, maybe restaurants or some kind of social club. "They have the German Association of Istanbul," I said. My husband was against it.

"We don't know what sorts of Turks they have here in Italy," he said. "Maybe nice, yes. Maybe like us, yes. Maybe, though, they are those lunatic Gülenists, or maybe, like in Germany, they all vote for Erdoğan so long as they don't live under his roof."

In the end, I agreed with him, not because of what he said, but because I wanted to be Italian now. If I was going to relocate my life, I wanted to invest in my new homeland in earnest. I wanted an Italian car, an Italian bank account, days along the Italian coast, and skiing trips in the Italian Alps. I wanted a circle of Italian friends.

"We don't know what sorts of Italians live around here," said my husband, nervous because of the stories we'd heard back home about how Italy and Spain, England and France treated migrants.

"Are we refugees?" I asked. "Come on. We've got cell phones and bank accounts and high heels and prescription medications."

"They'll think we're refugees. We don't know."

"We don't know many things," I said. He thought that

was hilarious and squeezed my hand hard just before stepping into the street without looking, and that little jolt, that sudden jump into the road made me shriek, so giddy was I with my husband in that moment. We spent the day, the week, the month walking the terraced alleys of Baronissi. It was a village of narrow streets reaching out in long, gentle curves like the nerves of a body toward the mountains beyond. While my father sat alone in his apartment under the guise of an independence that in fact he could no longer maintain, we offered up our meager but improving Italian to every shopkeeper we passed. I gained three kilos. Whenever I ran errands or went into town for coffee, I made a point to talk to as many people as I could, using all the new words I had memorized. My husband would joke when we went into Naples for a meal or a movie and I chatted with the waiter and the ticket-taker at the theater. "People will think you're nuts, Dilara. Don't you ever turn off?"

It wasn't that I had felt like I was being watched in Turkey, but becoming a stranger in an opaque country, I felt suddenly, entirely free from scrutiny. I think my husband did too, even if he still nursed his habitual suspicion.

It was difficult to gauge how he was adjusting to our new country. The thing that most effectively cracked his shell, like an oyster pried open into the cold sunlight, was the beach. We took frequent trips to the beaches all around Salerno, particularly Amalfi. He had grown up landlocked in Ankara, on that wide tableland raised up onto the shoulders of mountains, and when he moved to Istanbul, he told me he had spent weeks on the shore, standing on

the esplanade or visiting a café over the water or even hiring a fishing boat, which he didn't take out, just sat in it
bobbing happily against the pier—the dazzle of the sun
pricking against his eye, the shifting sounds of sea, the
strange tunnel-vision effect of the water across distances.
"A mountain," he said, "gets closer. The sea never gets
closer, no matter how far you climb into it." I got the sense
that, though he had been spellbound by the Bosporus,
there was not enough to maintain his interest—the soft
hills of Istanbul slipped into the water undramatically,
so unlike his histrionic, mountainous landscape. Now
in Italy, he was obsessed with the coast. The beaches at
Ravello, Positano, Amalfi—pebble-coarse slivers no wider
than an arm span—dived straight from the high cliffs into
the blue sea. The Mediterranean is different colors at its
different ports. In Istanbul the water changed at a whim,
but its habit was a light blue the color of dreams. Here
just south of Naples, the Mediterranean was a cool green,
a mossy, foggy shade like the undersides of all the vegeta-
tion growing in verdigris cascades down the faces of white
rocks, white cliffs. Here the villages were carved into the
rock, roads like the narrow steps up to the monastery bell
tower. Here the hills and mountains were deeply fissured
with pronounced spines, and colorful towns resting gently
in their niches—hidden. We walked the wide esplanade
along the coast under parasol cypresses. We walked the
shadow-doused alleys that folded in on themselves, that
climbed overtop each other and reached back like vines
gripping the narrow crevices of rock. We walked the steep
grade to cloisters carved into the faces of cliffs. We were

strangers, plucked out of our contexts, lost completely behind obscurity. Always there at the jagged shore was the dusky sea, our familiar companion. This was what I meant when I said I was a different person in Italy. The language, yes, changed us, but we had become something different as well, and I felt myself in love with a broader scale of life. I felt myself and my husband renewed in our happiness, and yes, perhaps it was because of the almost clinical extent of our isolation, like specimens in a petri dish, but this is a harsh light by which to consider it. We found ourselves free for devotion and redevotion—to each other, to happiness, but mostly to ease, if only briefly.

I looked online for school psychologist jobs in Naples. All that popped up was a course at the Institute of Relational Psychology. I called the institute to ask them if their program helped match students with careers afterward, but they told me I was overqualified to be a student. I expanded my search across all of Italy, but there were still only courses and programs, no actual jobs. I wrote directly to some professors and administrators, anyone whose email I could find, asking if they had any positions open or if they knew of any schools hiring. One replied saying that most schools had already finished hiring for the year and wouldn't start again until September.

I signed up to four different job databases, each one promising my future was a quick survey away and that dozens of companies with family-like cultures were just waiting for me to register my email to hire me. I uploaded my CV, then reiterated the same information in dialogue boxes, supplied my credit card information for the site subscription that I would have to cancel after the two-week free trial, and checked boxes for my field of study, my fields of experience, my fields of preference, my location, the hours I could manage, the languages I could speak, that I knew CPR, then I clicked Complete. This took half an hour or more for each database, and I felt my brain dribbling out of my ears. No companies messaged me right away, as each website had promised. Scrolling through the newest postings, I saw a few kitchen jobs and an office position at a waste management facility. I applied to the desk job. I checked my email inbox again, then I clicked around the database menus for a while. One had an interview prep page where you could practice with a chatbot.

Why do you want to work here?
   I've always wanted a break room.
What is your greatest strength?
   The time I lifted my father completely off the floor.
What is your greatest weakness?
   Chess.

I refreshed my inbox every ten or twenty seconds, until thirty minutes later, each of my new accounts received the same message from the hiring manager at a nearby accounting firm. The message was obviously written by AI, and promised a pay scale that rewarded tireless dedication and a go-getter's attitude.
   I closed the laptop and started going through the house

looking for loose change, paper bills tucked here and there, or else things I hoped would be there but weren't, like some gold jewelry I never wore, or an expensive watch my husband might have left behind, or a cell phone that we no longer used but was in near-mint condition. Instead, all I found were a box of one hundred envelopes (minus three or four) and six sheets of stamps. I used up all the printer paper printing CVs, filled the envelopes, and addressed them to the nearby coffee shops, restaurants, schools, utility companies, even the post office itself—everywhere in town I could think of. I took them to the post office, cramming unenveloped CVs into the letter box too, just to offload some of the dozens of spares. I even checked the coin return chutes in the two vending machines by the door on the way out, but nothing. Heading back through town I started slapping all the extra CVs on shop windows, or wrapping them around lampposts over other flyers, until I ran out. I wrote across the top of the last few: *Have you lost this psychologist?* Then put my number at the bottom.

Over the next few days, I watched a steady stream of women march past my door. Here were a dozen women already in the cells, and here were a dozen more coming down the hallway—tall women, short women, old women, young women, some in hijabs, some with quite fashionable hairstyles, some in rather expensive-looking athletic wear—and later there would be a dozen more, the same as before, each of them different from the next, not even unified in their expressions, some imperially stiff and self-satisfied, some faces mangled in fear. There were more guards too, though they were hardly around except to bring in new prisoners and leave again.

As newcomers went by, the other prisoners shouted out to them, saying: "Welcome, girlie, welcome to prison, what is new outside, what has happened since I last saw a sunrise, since I last saw a sunset?" I joined in with them. I didn't see any reason not to.

The guards bringing each new girl would tell us to hush up and stay in our beds until they were through, but after they tossed her into her cell, we immediately started shouting again: "What did you do to take a trip to prison?"

"Settle down," said a guard over the intercom in a voice so bored you'd think we were blades of grass.

I was always one of the loudest and most enthusiastic questioners, interrogating my new neighbor in a tone that—if these women didn't know me (which of course they didn't)—might be mistaken for jubilation.

"What did you do to take a first-class trip to prison?"

"Shut up, shut up, will you please shut up!" This was always Zeynep, the woman with the wide, wide face. Her cell wasn't that far from mine. It could've been the next one over. I never heard her cry. I heard some of the others cry, but not her. She made other sounds, fragile and whirring. I couldn't figure out what the noise was, and I didn't ask, but it was disconcerting all the same.

As more prisoners were brought in, the sounds of the women washed through my cell like a tide coming in and out through the days. I heard them turning in their cots like döner on the spit, or washing their faces and brushing their teeth, or what I could only guess was some sort of calisthenics across the floor. The prison's acoustics were strange and deceptive, and I found I could hear clearly a voice or a cough or a thump that must've been three, four, five cells away, or more, possibly all the way down the row!

I had stopped worrying about creating some fictitious crime to have landed me in prison. It was clear to me that I was no different from any of the women in there. What was my family doing in Italy, anyway? We had ostensibly left for my father, it's true. He was a dissident academic with a history of imprisonment, but I was a blacklisted psychologist with dubious political ties. What awaited me in Turkey? Where would I find myself now if I had stayed put in Istanbul and awaited my arrest like thousands of others? I could be right down the hall in a cell just like this one.

My father still wrote—even after the attempted coup, he wrote each morning. He drank a small cup of coffee to settle the night's dreams, then he went back to his old study, now refilled with his books and stationery, and closed the door. It was reassuring—he'd spent most of my childhood in that room, usually with the door closed but never locked, briefly distracted but never frustrated by my short-lived interruptions. His work was dull to me. There are few things more boring in life than watching a writer write. Throughout my youth, he existed as a low hum of labor in the household: the quiet click of his keyboard; the whispers of a pen on his students' papers; the scrape of his lighter—it made for a tickling, staticky shroud over the flat, something like a wool blanket. Now having returned to the flat, my father went right back to his desk, the hum of his work buzzed against the walls once more. This was a good sign, I thought. Stripped of his lectures and conferences and term papers, I wanted to keep his mind elastic any way we could.

"Is it such a good idea?" my husband asked. "Look at the rewards his last book earned us." But even with these fears written on his face, my husband agreed that mental exercise, regardless of its form, was good for my father. "I just wish he preferred sudoku."

I took to spying on my father. It was a way to make sure he was alright. Seeing him through the keyhole (yes, how complete the image of peeking!), hard at work on his computer—writing what might be his next novel, or maybe an academic paper, a lecture he might try to give as a visiting professor in some safer country—I told myself that nothing had changed.

His friend Berk was still coming around every other week, bringing news from the university. There had been a shift, no one could deny that. The political climate of the campus had been sharpening for years, but now—with the country under a state of emergency and special powers given over to the government—everyone was hunched with one eye over their shoulders. "They're replacing the rector," Berk told us. The first one in the university's history not appointed by the department heads but installed by government decree. "A friend of Erdoğan's son-in-law. The students protested, but the state of emergency . . ."

I didn't understand what was happening; Berk now trailed off, now missed opportunities to complain of the government. He seemed cowed, a smaller man than I remembered from one week to the next. Life in Turkey felt post-watershed, but what watershed? In my father's lifetime there had been two coups, six attempted coups, two near coups, three formal threats of coups that never happened, and who knew how many other thwarted plans for coups. There were protests in Turkey, always protests; there were killings in Turkey, always killings; there was martial law and curfews, and power-hungry generals, and governing by decree, and censorship laws, and insult laws, and laws that were good at landing unimportant people in jail and keeping important people out of jail, and there were mass arrests, and roundups, and indefinite detentions and trials and more trials, and trials without evidence, and verdicts without evidence, and general pardons and general panic—this was Turkey ever and always, an elected dictatorship, a Caesarian Rome, so why now did I get the sense that a threshold had been crossed, a boundary demarking before and after had been so completely transgressed?

In the evenings, as the three of us finished our dinner and gathered in the living room to unwind and have a little Scotch and a cigarette and some pistachios, we'd watch mindless television programs churned out for easy consumption. My father liked the old American ones, the mysteries I'd grown up with. We'd be halfway through a *Murder She Wrote* he'd seen a hundred times, and he'd ask who Angela Lansbury was playing or what the plot was for this episode. My husband looked at me. After a while we switched to *Columbo*, because the shows always started with the murderer. It wasn't a whodunit, but a howcatchem—I thought it'd be easier for my father. But still he'd turn to us with a straight face and say he thought the wife did it.

"We saw the murderer."

"It's the wife," said my father.

"It's the neighbor!" said my husband. We all were quiet after that, each tending our own private concerns.

Sometimes his comments went beyond mere confusion and he would say things that made no sense at all. One evening, very rationally, in the same tone he would use for one of his well-rehearsed lectures, my father said: "I'm scheming."

"What?"

"I'm scheming," he said in an unexpectedly intentional tone. "I'm taking my bike down to the shore to scheme."

"Did you ride your bike recently?" I asked. He didn't own a bike. I'd never seen him ride.

"Yes, that's how I got here."

My husband started shaking his head. All week he was shaking his head in disbelief. Disbelief at what but our own absurd lives.

Still I told myself things weren't so bad. It wasn't so bad to be in Turkey, despite the coup attempt, the mass purges and roundups and trials, getting fired, it wasn't so bad to be in Istanbul—there were always rough patches, things would turn around. History repeats itself so fast in Turkey, faster than in any other country. The return to our real lives was just around the corner; the erosions of democracy and the rule of law would be shored up once again; Erdoğan, as all strongmen in Turkey do, would face his fall—it was all just around the corner.

One late summer day in 2017, with the heat stretched, rippling over the sky, Berk came over to our flat without calling. He shoved past me at the door, apologizing but nonetheless frantic. He asked if I had any tea but before I could put the kettle on, he'd asked if I wouldn't mind running down to the corner shop for a pack of cigarettes. "I'm out," he said, patting his pockets. When I got back, he was pleading with my father about something. They hadn't heard me open the door so I listened, walking quietly to the kitchen but not actively sneaking, in case they should turn and see me and realize I had meant to eavesdrop. Two professors at the university had been raided that week— not just their offices but their homes too. A few others, having organized a protest of the new rector, were simply arrested without preamble, one in the middle of a lecture.

"I'm certain I'm next. My wife says the police came by our house this morning. If they're after me, they'll be after you too."

"Hmm," said my father.

"If I left . . . well, my family might not like it at first," said Berk. "Do you think yours would come around?"

"Left for where?"

"You and I could go to Greece."

I threw my keys onto the entryway table, and Berk turned away as if he were a child caught stealing chocolates.

"Dilara, do you think your husband would enjoy a trip to Greece?"

"Ha ha, have you been talking to him?"

"I was just telling your father it might not be a bad idea to go sailing."

Berk slapped my father's back and said he had to go. "Thank you for the cigarettes, Dilara. I'm sorry I'm not staying." He pulled me into the hallway after him, careful to be out of earshot of my father. He told me then very quickly that he'd been warned the police would be around to our place soon. If not today then within the week. "They collected up all the papers, books, computers, hard drives from our colleagues' offices," he said. "Nothing illegal, but there may well be emails implicating your father in who knows what." It was easy for them to find things, easier still to distort their findings. Berk told me that he was leaving for Albania at the end of the week. He wasn't even telling his wife. "If you want, I could bring your father with me. Just for a few months. This will all blow over soon enough. He and I could . . ." I think Berk realized even as he spoke that he couldn't take my father, couldn't bring a man in his condition along with him. In any case, I thought he was overreacting—sure, he might be arrested, but he'd soon be released again. People staged protests every day. And what would they arrest my father for? They

131

had had plenty of opportunity after his attack threw him into the local news spotlight. He was a pensioner with a failing memory. A threat to no one.

No, I told Berk he should go to Albania or Greece, just for a few weeks. Take in the sun and eat plenty of baklava. "It'll be alright."

"Yes," he said. "Of course."

Berk was arrested two days later. He is still, years later, in pretrial detention. I told my father after it happened and he didn't seem to understand. It was like he didn't even notice me talking. Then a moment later the reality of my words broke over him, and he gasped this hollow and defeated little laugh.

Yet even with Berk gone, this very close wound against my father, I did not seem to share in my family's gathering fear at our predicament. Then, three or five days later, days we should've spent packing, buying plane tickets, saying goodbye to relatives, settling debts and emptying accounts, my husband and I were washing up when my father appeared at the kitchen door asking for my mother. My husband and I exchanged looks.

"You mean Dilara?" I asked, offering him a chance to self-correct.

He called again into the silent kitchen, asking her to come out and eat with us. "Don't you love us, darling?"

He'd called me by my mother's name before. What parent hasn't called their children every name under the sun at some point? Growing up, he often called me my aunts' names, even sometimes the name of his childhood dog. And now and again, since our first visit to the hospital, he had called me Ayşe but immediately realized his mistake. This time was different. It wasn't a slip of the tongue. He looked into kitchen; he looked at me and saw my mother.

As the cells filled with women, the daily routine of the prison changed. I was in here after looking through my storage boxes for a new bristle pad, having yet again just washed the one oatmeal pot and two bowls my father and I had been using every day, when I heard a cell door open down the row and a guard commanding the woman in there to come out. Then I heard the guard walking down the line to another cell, this one closer to me, its occupant also marched out, and then another cell closer still. In a panic, I flew back to my flat, listening at my closed door but hearing absolutely nothing. I waited for fifteen, twenty minutes before poking my head back into the prison. I could hear a few women chatting nervously in neighboring cells. I pieced it together from their conversation: the cells had been emptied, at least half of the prisoners taken away. I waited at my door, watching for the guard, the first one I'd met, hoping he'd come down the hall so I could ask him what was going on. It wasn't long, a half hour or so later, the door at the end of the corridor clanged and the missing women were marched back down the row. I dove behind my partition, curled around the base of the toilet so that this time I could listen. The guards shouted a few commands as they slammed cells open and shut, their words difficult to discern in the clamor and echo. It sounded like some women were being put back into their cells while the others were being marched out. Were they being sent for interrogation? Torture? I waited until the guards were gone again and the row was still before disappearing back behind my bedroom door.

I was cautious as the next few mornings the practice repeated. Around the same time every morning, they came in and took half the women away for an hour, then came back to get the other half in turn. While I stayed curled up behind my partition listening, timidly trying to catch a few ends of conversations, a bit of information about what the guards were doing. Eventually, one afternoon, I decided to ask.

"Psst, psst," I said to the hallway. "Where did you go this morning? After breakfast?"

"Enough, eh. I'm sleeping."

"I didn't know. I can't see."

She made an exaggerated snoring sound.

"Where do you all go?"

"It's just exercise," she said, quitting her snoring sounds. Then, after a while: "What do you mean, where do we go? You're there."

"Yes," I said, panicking. "I was just checking it was the same for each group." I would need to be much more careful now there were other women in the prison, I realized. The first guard and the supervisor had made prison feel easy, a place where no one thought about you at all, where you became a part of the cell, invisible. Not so to the other prisoners. They would notice something strange immediately. They had nothing else to do but notice the place's rhythms and anything that disturbed them. I thought often about the guard, about the supervisor, about the trouble and the headache I would cause if people found out about my situation.

After that I adjusted my own routine so that I was conveniently absent whenever the prisoners were let out. The best time to visit the prison was late morning, after the women had returned from their exercise and were sitting on the rump of a new day, when they would start chatting, chatting in earnest, out of earshot from the guards. They asked each other about their dreams and offered up their meager divinations, which were always crude and artless and a bit on-the-nose. They spoke in idioms, like aunties at the village well, gossiping about ill children, weather patterns, the price of produce. I found myself the most talkative person in the bunch, but only just. You might think they'd be quiet types, stewing in their frustrations and resentments, but most of them were just scared of their futures, and we all approach that frightening shape in different ways. Some of the women talked nonstop, especially after a day or two of silence as a new arrival, a floodgate would open and then it was gab gab gab, though hardly any of it was interesting, to be honest. They were talking out their nerves, and though I tried to get them to open up about themselves, asking about their families, their work, the places they came from and the places they loved, they gave only superficial answers, as if there was nothing at all inside them.

But though they wouldn't discuss anything truly personal, they were often happy to gossip about the state of the country. I made a point of asking every new woman

135

what it was like in Turkey these days. I could read the paper, I wasn't actually trapped in prison, but life doesn't happen in the headlines. And without fail they told me that things were bad. They shouted back, with such confidence (how frightening to have such confidence!), that it was better to be in here right now anyway.

"The world and what it does to women, you wouldn't believe it!"

"Oh, sister, it is bad. I got three years for telling my neighbor I had to raise my prices for inflation. I should've kept it to myself."

"That's nothing," a young girl replied. "Aunties, I promise I wasn't doing anything at all, and I was arrested for saying that I couldn't afford tomatoes."

They all agreed that they were being arrested for smaller and smaller infractions. Of course, I had to account for the hyperbole of prisoners and their claims of innocence. Some of them didn't mind telling the whole row that they were in there for stealing from their employer; for kidnapping a cousin's child; for being choked by their brother, throttled by him, and in a foggy and delirious moment stabbing him before he could kill them. But mostly these were women who had been at protests, or written emails to their local representatives, or worked for the wrong newspapers, or studied at the wrong schools, or spoke the wrong languages—subversives.

Take for example the grandmother and granddaughter who arrived one morning: they were brought through the hallway handcuffed to each other. The policeman had barely snapped the cuffs closed, he must have been rushing to get on to the next arrest, and they dangled uselessly off the wrists of the girl and old woman. They had to keep sliding them up their forearms, eventually giving up and holding one cuff each in their hands like a dog leash. They didn't mind the loose handcuffs, and the police and guards didn't either; they were just a grandmother and granddaughter out for a stroll.

The girl said often: "I'm not really in prison myself. I'm not a criminal anyway."

Though many of the women in the prison said that, what she meant was that she personally had not been arrested, arraigned, and held in pretrial detention; rather her grandmother had. Her grandmother was Kurdish, from a small, rural village, and could not speak Turkish. When her health waned, she moved to the city to live with her daughter's family. She went to the grocer and the café and the pharmacist, speaking Kurdish and pointing to everything she wanted. Someone turned her in as a terrorist sympathizer. The state of emergency and the martial law like a shroud over the eastern cities made it difficult to keep track of what was a language and what was an act of violence.

The police said: "Why don't you speak Turkish?"

She said: "There's no emergency, thank you. I'm living with my daughter and her family."

But they didn't understand Kurdish. They looked through the house, finding the girl studying in the kitchen, and demanded she translate. The girl did as she was told and the police had her explain they were going to take her grandma into the station. They warned her that they didn't have an interpreter.

"That's okay," said the girl. "I'll come along."

They cuffed them both and took them to the station. "Sorry, miss," the police said to the girl, "you have to be cuffed to ride in the back." They jailed them together, having the girl translate everything so the grandma couldn't get out of this on some legal technicality (and the police must have thought themselves very clever to account for this). The two of them were awaiting trial in detention as evidence was gathered, but that could take years, and the jails were full so they were put in this prison, the girl here as a permanent interpreter, stuck to her grandmother like a tumor, and just like a tumor suffering the same fate as the rest of the body.

I called the garage where my husband worked and left them a voicemail about my predicament. Well, I told them my husband had broken his leg and would be bedridden for six weeks, and that we would appreciate greatly a month or two's wages in advance while he healed. I said I hoped they would understand. Then I decided to condense the two bank accounts my husband and I shared into one to avoid the extra service fees. I thought about texting my husband to warn him that one of the cards wouldn't work anymore, but I could see he hadn't been using either of them since he left anyway. I had just got off the phone with the bank and was about to make a quick lunch when my father appeared with three petals of blood on his fingertips. For years now, my father had suffered these little sores all over his arms and legs. The body takes much longer to heal as it ages. It remembers more than the mind does. They were perpetually scabbing, these wounds, and sometimes they would start to bleed again, and I'd scold him for picking at them, though I never caught him doing so and he always said he hadn't touched them. I don't know where they came from. It didn't take much—a quick turn (quick for his age) and his wrist would hit the edge of a counter or table, and then he'd have a scab there for a year.

I spent the rest of the morning stanching a few new lesions and checking the old ones for infection. On his palm I found a burn blister. "How did this happen?" I asked.

"What?"

Then I dragged his chair to a spot by the window (he wasn't happy in front of the TV anymore). The thing weighed well over fifty kilos with all its bells and whistles, the mechanism which tilted it backward and raised the footrest and swiveled the whole contraption on its base. By the time I got him set up in his new spot and then through the routine of doling out his medications, feeding him some lunch so he didn't vomit the meds back up, and finally set about cleaning the kitchen, it was late afternoon. I took a deep breath and walked out of the flat, down to the garage, and got in my car.

When I arrived at Lucia and Giovanni's house, I must have looked feral. My last shower was three, five days ago.

I'd been peeling and heating so many frozen dinners that my forefinger had a permanent sticky patch on it from the cellophane glue on the packaging, and as I wiped the sleep from my eyes, the grit stuck to my glue finger.

My friends pulled me into their apartment. I don't think I had ever entered any other way. Lucia and Giovanni were the sort of people who, almost pugnaciously, impressed their friendship quickly and completely on others. In fact, that was true of most people we had met in Italy. Sometimes I thought that was what had drawn us here to begin with. I couldn't imagine how miserable we'd have been in the Netherlands or Denmark, surrounded by humorless and reclusive characters (though I'd never met anyone from northern Europe, so what did I know?).

They sat me down at the kitchen table and brought me a glass of water, and Lucia began putting together a tray of pastries and fruit while Giovanni started up the espresso machine. I apologized for just showing up; I hadn't meant to barge in like this. They reassured me immediately, it was no trouble, they were delighted to see me, and I noticed both of their voices and even their body language were very gentle but firm, the way you would speak to someone having a panic attack, and only after realizing this did I notice my shortness of breath, the precise and biting pain behind my right eye, the tremors of the muscles in my arms. They did their best to talk me down. They said I would stay right here and relax, help Lucia decide on a wine list for her sister's party. They said that I already looked better. The color was coming back to my face. They told me everything was alright, Giovanni would call the garage and let my husband know I was here, that he could come by after work and join us for coffee.

"He's not at the garage."

"Oh, is he at home then? Well, we can drive you back when you feel ready, that's no problem. Gian will take your car and you'll ride with me."

No, he wasn't home. "He's up north. He had to take a seasonal job at a different garage."

Lucia flashed a look at Giovanni so quick I hardly noticed. She opened her mouth to ask another question but nothing came out, so she yawned and went to grab a dish of sugar cubes while Giovanni brought our espressos to the table.

"I can't go back. Not yet," I said. "I can't breathe." I could breathe, of course. I was speaking, after all, but I had the sense that if I were to get up now and walk back to my car, my breath might actually stop. I couldn't go back to my father just yet, now that I was away from him. "But Dad is alone."

"Gian will go check on him," Lucia said.

"I just made coffee, huh." She gave him a sore look and he stood up. "Of course, I will go look in on him."

Lucia started pulling out cheeses and cured meats, asking me to sample them and help her decide which would be best for a party. Her sister-in-law had recently had her third child and Lucia was hosting the christening reception. It was calming to hear her little issues (the wine she preferred was unavailable, the cheese was too crumbly, they hadn't enough table covers for the rented high-tops).

I felt myself being swept up into a life very far away from my own, in the irresistible energy of my friend, her speech running so fast I had trouble keeping up. Lucia often sounded a bit frantic, but with her it wasn't always unwarranted. She had a taxing job at an architecture firm and an extended family that took advantage of her financial stability as often as they were in legal trouble. I carried on listening to her stories, occasionally asking her to slow down. By the time we had finished the peppered salami and washed it down with wine enough to blush my cheeks and make my head feel precariously balanced on my shoulder, I had uncoiled months' worth of tension from my jaw, neck, back, arms, legs. And even then, Lucia kept bringing out more snacks, little chocolates and other delicate desserts, placing them right into the palm of my hand and then taking my other hand in hers as I ate, pressing it earnestly, as if she were relishing the chocolate through me. I never saw her eat sugar.

I probably should not have driven myself home. The wine was in my eyes on the sharply curved roads, but hardly anyone was out so early in the evening. When I pulled up to the building and climbed the stairs to my flat, I found my father sitting across the tavla board from Giovanni. "Ah, you're back. See, your daughter is back now."

"What's he say?" my father asked.

"Thank you, Giovanni. I'm sure there are better ways to spend your afternoon."

Giovanni stood and clapped my father's shoulder,

smiling very large, so large a smile it might fall off his face. "Nonsense. We had fun, didn't we, old man?"

"Fuck off."

"That's right, he's very good. I don't think he would've let me win if I begged."

"Go away, go away," said my father. "I can't stand it."

"What did he say?" said Giovanni.

"What's he say?" said my father.

I thanked Giovanni again. He said he would make sure that Lucia called more often, that he would come over to watch the old man if I ever needed another moment for myself. "Maybe, if your husband calls while I'm around, I can talk to him. It's not good taking a job so far from you two." I hugged Giovanni, and wanting to send him home with something but not having made anything myself in weeks, I tucked a frozen dinner container under his arm.

Growing up, everyone called me little Ayşe, minik Ayşe. I had been shown so many photographs of my mother as a child—her side of the family was obsessed with taking pictures and hoarding them for posterity; practically her whole childhood had been captured in meticulous detail— and the resemblance between us was obvious even to me.

On days of boredom, seeking distraction, my mother would take me by the hand into my father's study, to the desk drawers that were crammed overfull with those cheap, three-by-five photo albums that come complimentary from the developer. "Come, let's read my pictures," she said. My father, who'd been reading in his chair or writing at the desk when we brushed past him, upending his work, chimed in regularly: "You can't read pictures."

"Mom can. She reads them to me."

These albums documented entirely mundane events, often a whole album dedicated to a single ordinary outing, with each photo taken minutes or even moments after the last one. In this way they tracked, for example, a family walk through the neighborhood almost in stop-motion. My mother kept these sequences carefully intact, never removing the pictures from their sleeves; each had a narrative: this was a day trip to her father's relatives in Moda; this was one morning on vacation in Bodrum; and here another trip to Moda, separated from the first by thirty-some years. My mother wore white dresses with little white ribbons in her hair in so many of the photos that it was like a uniform, an outfit I also wore consistently between the ages of two and eight. As a child, my mother had wind-racked, light brown hair, as did I. We both had clumsily large noses, heavy-lidded eyes set far apart, and long, knobby legs. When we smiled—our faces all squashed up like that—we were practically indistinguishable, we might have been the same girl on different days, the time lapse given away only by a handful of newer cars parked on the streets, fresher coats of paint on the row of houses, larger pieces of furniture piled into the same rooms.

Little Ayşe, minik Ayşe. Through grade school and then high school all my relatives called me by my mother's name or, to distinguish us, called me just Minik. Then she died and no one called me that anymore.

It was strange to think about her death. It came and went too fast; we didn't experience it. I was left with so unsatisfyingly little of the event that I had to reconstruct it afterward, coaxing the details from my relatives—first in an effort to convince myself that she was really gone, and then as part of the much slower task of understanding the loss of her. Were there any auguries of her death coming like gray birds in migration? I don't know why we hadn't been better prepared. We should have expected the tragedy, in a family of many widows and widowers, as if loss were a recessive gene. She was sick and then dead in a week. With my father it was the opposite. Death was here in the corner of the room, or even closer, strapped to his neck like the tube of an oxygen tank, but still we had to eat our dinner, still we had to decide on a TV show to watch—I was constantly unmaking his death—who could live otherwise? I'd had to make a death for my mother because she died so fast, and now I was trying to make a life for my father as he was swallowed in unending decline.

I remembered my mother in brief vignettes that shine golden in the darkness of my mind's eye—her voice and her perfume, how it felt to stand beside her, the shape of my arms when they hugged her. I had pictures of her as an adult too, of course, many of them taken by me. My mother with her sisters in our kitchen; her and my father reading in the sitting room; a whole album of her alone, sitting in the wingback chair by the window, the terrifyingly large window. I was quite young and not an especially skilled photographer—the camera's light meter was registered on the window, producing a roll full of our neighbors' buildings, a shallow sky, and a few treetops, with a black chunk missing in the shape of my mother.

In retrospect it felt like I hardly knew her. What plans had she made of her life, how happy was she, how proud was she of our family, were there regrets, were there blunders, were there moments of complete helplessness? Was my mother a person under the label of "mother"? Of course she was but I hadn't ever met her, not really, not after I myself had grown up and lived these things too. I needed my father to reconstruct her for me, fill her in from my limited scaffolding. So many little memories of her he had! And he shared them with me every day after her death. I saw this injured him, but I couldn't help myself. I demanded more—more happy trinkets, intricate filigrees, clever tales, and secret gardens. From all of these I was able to build a palace and fill it with bright, wonderful things: leftover baklava syrup mixed with tea; a finger slightly pickled from plucking olives out of martinis; the soft shush of her voice without words; thistle-colored evenings and sweet-scented cigarettes.

But the palace was fast dilapidating if I did not, every few months, ask my father to repeat a story I had heard before: the two of them sleeping overnight in the Ankara train station as students, or how they had, pretending to be offended, stormed out of my paternal grandparents' place out of sheer boredom. I begged for new details to enrich these familiar images and he obliged when he could, but perhaps the first memories he started losing were those of her. Of course it's impossible to know either way. He might have lost others too, ones I did not or could not notice in the midst of our semi-estrangement. I had on my mind only our singular point of connection: my mother. Always, he said *Yes, of course, I miss her too*, and then smiling he began telling me how she would steal small bills out of his wallet before he left for work. He took longer and longer to produce each new offering, however, and he began repeating them even when I hadn't asked him to (forgivable, I demanded so much and a person contains only so many stories), and perhaps this was part of why we both allowed the distance to swell between us in those years before Gezi Park brought us back together. I should have been more concerned, though, when he began asking me for information, for stories, for secrets. Occasionally, he came to me with an empty bag, palm upturned, and asked if I had anything precious of my mother to share. In those moments, a terrible jealousy struck me. How greedy I was! Angry, I would leave my father's flat. The poor man. I did not consider that he only wished to partake in a joint ritual of remembering, nor did I consider what I now think was most likely: a leak had sprung in the side of him, and the font had started dribbling out, as irreparable as water seeping into desert sands.

I had been spending a lot of time going through my old graduate psychology textbooks. God knows why I had held on to them when we moved to Italy, but after a few days of trying to get the prisoners to open up to me, with limited success, I thought they might be a useful resource. I hadn't really exercised my skills in years and felt rusty looking back over notes and chapters on building trust. I had worked a lot with nonverbal kids, using communication boards or gestures or inventing our own rudimentary sign language. You had to build a safety net of silence, you put images in front of them and ask them what they want to do, so they point to a kid either kicking a ball or a playing a board game or eating a pizza. I laughed thinking of sitting in front of these prisoners, pointing to drawings of hamburgers and basketballs. The principles were the same, though, you're supposed to show them you're trustworthy very slowly, and here I was shouting with the others at the newcomers.

After I exhausted the information in my textbooks, I thought there might be some resources online for people who teach literature or woodworking in prisons, articles or tips for engaging with the incarcerated, convincing them you were a safe and stable aspect of their lives. I combed the internet but in the end I realized this search was even less relevant than my child psychology notes—most of the women I was dealing with were not, in any real sense, criminals.

Meanwhile the open tabs of job descriptions went ignored. Occasionally, while I scrolled through an interview with a former inmate or skimmed an article on the long-term psychological effects of imprisonment, my email would ding with a response to a job application I had absent-mindedly sent off. I couldn't face opening it to read yet again I wasn't the right candidate. Maybe the unread emails didn't say that; maybe I had been offered an interview with a good company that paid a decent salary, and I would read the message again and again to make sure it was a promising position and start scripting what I would say about my time away from the workforce, and find someone to watch my father, and on the way home from my note-perfect interview I would then giddily fantasize about the hospice worker I could afford for my father, the nights out into town or up to Naples I would spend eating silky heaps of burrata and sweet, peppered tomatoes, and drinking a dry, very dry martini, lunar almost in its excellence, and then offering the glass to my husband just to watch his face screw up when he sipped the gin. Well, he wouldn't be there I guess, but still a night out would do me good, a fat meal that sticks in lardy lumps to the ribs would do me good, before coming back home and giving my father one two three types of pills, washing them down with a hot chocolate, getting up in the morning and helping him rinse his face, rinse under his arms, explaining to him that a nice woman was coming to visit while I would be out at work and yes I am leaving early and yes I am returning late but this nice woman knows all your medications and she is very kind and patient and speaks a little Turkish too . . .

Rooting around in my storage boxes for a tea towel, I came upon an old hard drive from when we first arrived in Italy. As soon as I caught sight of it, I knew: this was the hard drive that held my missing photographs, the ones

I took on our last night in Istanbul. A soft whoosh swept up the hairs of my arm like a petting breath. I suddenly felt a scintillating wave of expectation—like stepping into an ancient room closed off for so many years, the kind that can tumble you back, back, all the way back, to your youth—everything much smaller than you remember.

I darted out of the cell, retrieving my laptop from where it lay on my bed, and brought it back in. Plugging in the hard drive with my hands almost shaking, I opened the folder—sure enough, among so many other, now superfluous files, the thumbnails of the pictures drew my eye. But as soon as I enlarged them, I realized something was wrong. They were full of misplaced details, almost nothing like I had remembered. It was like one of those spot-the-difference games. I had only recalled one other couple in the restaurant, but the picture showed the patio packed with people at every table, the restaurant full to capacity, some tables even crowded with extra chairs. The umbrellas over the tables were too big, the plates and glassware were piled up, and then the top of the frame was cropped tight around the trees so that the sky was butted out by things, things, things. The lone waiter was still there, at least, and he still wore a black waistcoat with a black tie, and white shirtsleeves, and a little white apron. He balanced on one hand a small tray of delicate glasses and three porcelain cups. With the other hand, he gave a short tug on the tablecloth, returning it to a perfectly smooth surface. He placed the thin saucers with their cups on the linen. On one side of the table were my maternal aunts and uncle, all in sunglasses, all smiling, all facing out to sea; on the other were my cousins, their girlfriends, my husband and father. There was no sense of conspiracy in the composition, none of that youthful and giddy secrecy my mother and I had invented over our many visits. My family was there in its entirety. It was a photograph of our goodbye, after all—so why had I expected whispers and finger sandwiches, giggling and torturous gossip? Why had I expected to see my mother?

The other picture also looked wrong. The "German couple" were not old but young, and almost certainly not German. They were sharing a torte, the woman reaching, plucking at a knuckle hair on the man's hand, the man with his mouth closed, evidently chewing, the Bosporus beyond them a simple edge, silver in the setting sun, silver to match the water goblets frosted with condensation. Little yachts and fishing boats bobbed at the shoreline. Cafés and boutiques dotted the inlet before them, and at the opposite shore all the mansions stood in the resplendent light of a multicolored afternoon. The heavy scent of coffee fell over me, and the faint sound of pastry flaking under a knife rustled in my ear. A far-off horn, a boat departing. Gulls moving like ghosts at the edge of the world. I became small as a sensation, suddenly surrounded by everything. The waiter was just now setting silverware at my place, and with a silent and precise motion, he produced a pen and pad from his pocket and asked what I would like to order, and I thought I should have a bit of orange juice. I couldn't think of anything else, as if that was the only thing in the world to me, the only color missing from all this white, all this azure, all this silver, all this green covering the restaurant overlooking the sea. Orange juice, as orange as the morning. I felt young, peeled clean of all my years. As if telepathically, my uncle told the waiter that I'd like orange juice in a voice much younger than himself, and my aunts laughed a bout of laughter much younger than themselves. I felt something pulling through me, a bit of string tied around the root of my tongue and stretching down my throat to my stomach—it was yanked, yanked, yanking me away from the patio. I stood from the table, left the waiter and my family, and jumped away from the restaurant, deaf to the tinkling sounds of teacups and wineglasses, deaf to the gulls and the low rumble of traffic—quick step off the terrace and straight back into the prison cell, another quick step back to my room in Baronissi and diving into my bed. How absolutely hollowing this gulf—all the world between myself and myself and I was cored, blind in the chasm of difference.

I tried to find the restaurant online, using the scenery in the two photographs for reference. In the background, the inlet was gently curved with a small mosque at its apex, a little minaret. It was evening, the sun casting shadows from the west, so the camera must be facing south toward the bridge over the water, but no matter how many times I clicked the map interface up and down the Bosporus, the landmarks were incongruent, disjointed, or else not even there. Not only did the inlet not exist, but the way the skyline was, with certain palaces here and a mosque there, the whole image seemed to be impossible—completely fabricated!

There were just the two pictures, yes, but over time, I'd

made them the foundations on top of which I had laid so many remembered events into tidy, ordered narratives— and mine were counterfeit. What would happen to me if I kept interrogating photographs and maps and found them contradictory to yet more of my memories? Would they shatter into a thousand pieces, every one of them a tomb?

When we emigrated, something about my dad's condition, something about how he conflated the present with the past, kept me feeling safe—like we were bringing a little of the old Istanbul with us. It wasn't so bad to leave the apartment I had grown up in, it wasn't so bad to become an exile, it wasn't so bad that our homeland was in ruins, because we had with us a little old man carrying its halcyon days in a kerchief on a stick. His voice came from before all the loss. The way he talked was a bridge to our lives left behind. Maybe that is what we do—the children, I mean: we make our parents into portals.

Many things changed in Turkey, but they didn't affect him. They renamed the Bosporus Bridge a few days after the coup attempt. People thought it was an act of remembering, of honoring. Truly it was a forgetting. The way a state orchestrates memorials is the same way that it orchestrates forgettings. Possibilities are limited when a country organizes its memory. Until we left, I had not noticed how easily state architecture conspires against the people. Indeed, I doubted I would recognize Istanbul at all anymore. The country was changing—quickly, quickly. I heard from friends I desperately wished had fled like me, that the streets were shedding their small, family-run shops to make way for glitzy new banks, new chain cafés and restaurants. The verdigris hills had gone over to cheap apartments, gaudy hotels, skyscrapers casting phallic shadows over the city. The shore, once a brilliant and inviting lapis, disappeared behind a curtain of construction. All the gardens and parks of the city, once protected as green spaces by law, were being sacrificed to the unyielding current of progress. Progress!—always a shout, a shout of death! So too were the infrastructures of the people being eroded: the newspapers and TV programs dwindling, and the journalists and artists going into their prisons with satisfied frowns, and the lira plummeted, and refugees grew in number and desperation, and the places shed their true names, hardly noticed as phases of the moon—and my father was immune to all of it.

Even if I showed it all to him, even if I sat him down in front of the computer and showed him article after article, photograph after photograph, nothing would penetrate that shell that protected the Istanbul of his past. I started thinking of him as a walking, breathing time capsule, a point on the axis of time plucked out of its station. He still held his separate Istanbul like a stone in his palm, apart from me and the rest of the world. Soon this too would go. My father's head was getting lighter. His brain was shrinking the way a sponge dries into a brittle form. What parts of him have already evaporated? What is the weight of a memory?

It had been many days since I had seen anyone but a guard in the corridor when a new woman was brought in one evening, just before lights-out, when there was usually a calm and drowsy atmosphere. She was much younger, very thin; if you squinted, she might have been mistaken for a broom or a sapling. The guard marched her past my door, winking a threat at me as he passed. They stopped just out of sight and the guard jangled his keys. She was going into the cell next to mine. After the guard shut her in and walked off, I heard at once an odd purring coming from my new neighbor.

"Hello, hello, deary!" I said, wishing I had my mother's natural hospitality and warmth instead of my own jumping awkwardness. "I mean welcome. I mean, I am glad you're here. Well, no . . . I mean . . ."

"She doesn't want that!" shouted Zeynep, cutting the little line of connection I had been unspooling down the hall. "She doesn't want to hear you right now. I don't want to hear you right now. Shut up!"

I could always recognize Zeynep's voice, though she spoke relatively rarely—the sound of it seemed to crawl right out of the concrete around me and down into my ears. It made the silence after even quieter, as if her shouting had deafened me. I stayed put for a while, struck dumb and listening but hearing nothing. I needed to go home anyway, to make a meager meal for my father, to see if the garage where my husband had worked had returned my call. I needed to turn down the heat in my flat though it was January. I had a timetable taken from the internet about how to maximize energy savings. I needed to cancel the internet. But I couldn't lift my feet from the floor. A buzzer sounded at the end of the hall, then a click, or a door closing—they would shut out the lights soon. I had never stayed in the prison after dark, it was something that for no good reason frightened me, artificial as the night and day were in there, but I didn't want to take any chances. In fairy tales, the magic shifts at dusk, the pumpkin reforming at the stroke of midnight.

Then a little voice: "Are you there, please?"

I hesitated. "Yes, I'm here. Are you there?"

"Please don't hurt me," said the girl.

"Hurt you?"

"I'm sorry. I'm sorry. I told the guard I was sorry, too."

"I'm not sorry," said Zeynep.

"Please," said the girl. "I shouldn't be here. I'm not a criminal."

"I'm not a criminal," said Zeynep.

"I'm not a criminal, either," I said, trying to sound different than Zeynep, more truthful, though this was unfair of me.

The girl fell silent.

"What's your name?" I asked.

"Please. You won't hurt me. You won't hurt me . . ." She wept, pleading. I didn't know what to say, even Zeynep had retreated into her silence, and so I whispered *hush, hush* to the girl as she cried. She wouldn't be able to hear my voice over the sound of her own tears but I murmured anyway, *hush, hush*, and I stayed listening to it all. The lights in my cell went out, and the girl kept crying, and I wanted to run and run, away, through the door into my bedroom, out of the bedroom into the hall, out of the hall into the stairwell, out of the stairwell into the evening with its early lamplights now twinkling and the ribbon of the Milky Way right there, just beyond the eye's reach, but still I stayed. Eventually she sobbed herself tired and fell asleep. Her halting, troubled breaths filled the space between us, collecting against the bars the walls the floor the ceiling, all of it so dense and unforgiving. The patter of her sleeping grew and was joined gradually by the drowsy rustling of other women slipping under their sheets, and at last the trance broke and I escaped.

My father surprised me at the doorway as I was sneaking back into the bedroom.

"Why have you moved the chair?" he demanded.

"You wanted it by the window," I said.

"It was never there. It was in the back room, not this one."

I walked him to the only sitting room in our apartment and pointed to his chair and told him this was a different flat. We weren't in Istanbul anymore. I said it like I wanted to hurt him with this information, and regretted it immediately because I could see his tangle of thoughts come loose and reorganize themselves for a moment.

"I know we're not in Istanbul," he shouted at me. "I know it every day, because I am miserable here. You have kidnapped me and taken away my family and for what? Why do you hate me, huh?"

"I don't hate you," I said.

"You do."

"I don't."

"That's why you have moved my chair. And you don't listen. And you've changed the hallway now!" The spool came undone. He was in our old flat again. I turned to the fridge to gather our dinner: a few meatballs, tomatoes and cheese, a half piece of pita.

"Dad, you have to eat something."

"I ate," he said distrustfully.

"You must eat something more than a baked potato and some popcorn. Come on. That's why you feel sick all the time."

"I'm not sick."

"Dad."

"Stop calling me that. I'm not your father. I don't know who your father is."

I sighed because we'd done this before. I had, in the past, tried to convince him it was me, his daughter. It never went anywhere. "You're important to me," I said.

He thought for a while, or at least looked like he was thinking. Sometimes it was hard to tell what was going on in these pauses that seemed like an actor getting into character, but then never delivering his lines.

"You're someone who is important to me too, aren't you?" he said at last.

"Eat up."

"This is not correct."

I sometimes think about his soul. Not some poetic thing, but as close as one could get to a scientific description. I think whatever it is must be the thing dementia takes away. What remains is this vessel that is my father, that looks like him and smells like him, but is completely empty. He can't interact with his surroundings anymore. He is digging and digging and digging through the mines of himself to find a fragment of meaning, and I convince myself that so long as this is happening, he still has his soul, but what will it mean when the mine is exhausted? When he is a corpse that still breathes, still sees—what will I do then?

How much it hurts to watch someone dissolve beneath their own skin.

PART IV

HOW HAD I FOUND myself lying on the cot in the prison cell when I had meant to grab a little paprika for my omelet? It was hard to explain. I had begun waking in the early morning and climbing out of my normal bed, and quickly shuffling into the cell, crawling onto the cot to "wake up" a second time in there. I would stay there for a spell just breathing the prison air—constricted, fateless. Have you ever sat very still in an open field? Have you ever lain on your back with grass stalks bending beneath you and a blue sky, so blue the color falls into your eyelashes, crowding out your eyes and not letting anything else in, the sense of belonging echoing up from the dirt through your skin? You call it transcendence or the sublime, but it is just harmony, I think. It's hearing the invisible sea while you fall asleep. It is all the inside lights of your body shutting off in deference to the moon. It was a sensation of peace so all-encompassing that I felt a hole had been dug out in the earth for me and I had been placed into it and covered over again.

I would do something similar at the end of the day, resting in the darkness until the women had stopped talking for the night before finally leaving for my own bed. I was about to rouse myself and go home, when Zeynep called out to me, asking if I still wanted to know how she ended up here. Surprised, I said I did, and she told me she was imprisoned because of something she said to a fellow reporter.

In fact I knew this already, because after I learned her name and her job, I had looked her up. It took a little while to find the right Zeynep, but there are not so many journalists in Turkey named Zeynep, and fortunately for me her case had been quite public. She had, over the course of her career, covered a number of incendiary topics, like the rise of femicide rates in the first decade of Erdoğan's rule (1,400 percent) and the court judges systematically reducing sentences for domestic abuse. She had profiled the women behind the Saturday Mothers group, the demonstrations in the wake of Özgecan Aslan's murder, and the People's Democratic Party. She had penned op-eds against government statements like: *You cannot make men and women equal*, and *Women should not laugh in public*. And then when the AKP pulled Turkey out of the Istanbul Convention on domestic violence, something they had been threatening to do for years, Zeynep had published a column attacking the withdrawal. A reporter from the state-run press agency tracked her down at a protest and asked her on camera: "Do you think it's hard to be a woman?"

"No, I do it every day. What appears to be difficult

is for others to approach my existence as a woman with compassion."

"And do you think that's true in Turkey?"

"I think that's true everywhere."

"There you have it," said the reporter, turning back to the camera. "Turkey is no better and no worse than the rest of Europe in its treatment of women. Since the withdrawal from the Istanbul Convention—"

"Hold it," said Zeynep. "I didn't say that. No, no, no, Turkey is bad for women. It is worse than many other places. It is a state infested with misogynists. The current regime is a political system built upon the exploitation and oppression of women."

"Are you confessing?" the reporter asked.

"What?"

"Are you confessing to a crime?"

"What crime?"

"It is a crime to denigrate the Republic," said the reporter. "To be against the state."

"If it is a crime to be against the state, and the state is against women, then I have no say in my existence as a crime."

I knew all this, but I let Zeynep tell me the story anyway. She became angrier and angrier as she spoke, her words flying so fast they caught sometimes on the corners of her mouth. "A woman is nothing without her family, so they think. The family must be protected, they say, and I said that their *family* was endangering women, maiming them, strangling them, killing them. They say women's rights erode family unity, but actually it's violence that destroys families, unchecked violent abuse, which the AKP are more than happy to allow! They call any divorced or unmarried woman a prostitute, yet they don't talk about the hatesome boys who, because they are not given everything on a platter, are not treated as sultans, think it is well within their rights to shoot someone point-blank!" This, too, had been covered in the news, even in Italy—a man in Ankara who murdered his fiancée because she broke off their engagement. "To be a man in Turkey is to become inhuman. A creature entirely without love. So that is why I am here like a criminal. They brought me in after the TV clip, that same evening. I got five years in prison by the end of the week."

A few other women who had not yet fallen asleep began chiming in with their own tales of arrest, many of which I had heard before, talking about how they were blithely minding their own business, and how, if they ever got out of here (they swore up and down to God about this), they would never be so blithe again.

I listened for a while but I found the other stories tiresome. I didn't want to hear these things; I really didn't care about their misfortunes, which were like a hiccup in the heart. In truth I wanted to hear about their neighborhoods, their cities and villages. I wanted them to tell me about the new restaurants in Bebek and the old ones that had stayed afloat. Had they smuggled a piece of pistachio marzipan into the prison and to share, morsel by indulgent morsel, with me? Had their relatives, when they were allowed to visit the prison, brought a few packs of Turkish cigarettes, tea from Rize, a twist of simit? I wanted these women to pick up old conversations with me, and reveal that they were my friends from my university days, friends who had made it through turbulent times unscathed and still aglow. I wanted these women to say, "Oh my, how we've missed you, but of course everything is fine now; please return at once, please return to your flat at the top of the street, and we'll throw you a never-ending party with enough champagne to turn us golden and sparkling." I wanted what I could no longer get from my father.

I knew their dreary tribulations would be the same as my own if I were ever to return to Turkey. Indeed, I was in Turkey now; I was in the very prison they would send me to if I ever alighted from the plane and produced my passport. Why think about it? Better to dream of the marzipan from my favorite baker in Kuruçeşme, rich and so unbelievably fine, and even as I recalled it, I noticed a plate bearing five rolls of the very same marzipan waiting on the table in my cell, and I ate them up quickly, knowing they could not be saved for later. Whatever it was about the prison cell that answered my wishes in an instant, it never lasted. If I turned my back on the marzipan, I knew, it would have disappeared by the time I looked around again. And if I tried to bring it home with me, first the flavor would drain out of it, then the sandy texture, grain by grain, would evaporate until the rolls were completely gone. Anything I ever took from the cell had a way of fizzling out of my sight, without me noticing exactly, coming undone at the seams in my peripheral vision.

Returning from my cell always left a strange residue

on my skin, like confectioners' sugar stuck to a smear of sweat. I used to be the sort of person to shower after a little gardening or dishwashing, but I enjoyed the feeling of it, the misty, gritty coating all over me, diesel and sea salt close on the collar like a tickling spell. Besides, minutes later, inspecting my hands and arms and face, I would find the residue gone anyway, and I'd smell just like my old self.

When there is something missing from you, how do you fill the space? Walks through your neighborhood? Flipping through old photos? Calling friends, lovers, relatives and talking about the old days? Do you describe the boundary of the void obsessively, or simply cover its shapelessness with a veil? Over time, I determined that it was better not to get mixed up in the nonsense of the other prisoners. It was better to spend my hours just sitting quietly in my cell, as the fog that choked out my old life gradually dispersed. My thoughts sharpened then, rattling around and setting off other thoughts in a thousand brilliant directions. I felt pleasurably scattered across myself, remembering everything so clearly, so much of my mother, so much of my city, my friends, my family, my father before his dementia. I remembered it all, but only in the way that in dreams we can speak other languages or have learned the trick of flight—it *feels* true but there is no root under the soil. In those moments I was experiencing the sensation of remembering, that gratifying and jubilant sensation of click, click, click, but afterward I couldn't say what I saw, what I heard, what I smelled—there was nothing. As with all the cell's gifts, the droplets of memory fell away as soon as I left the room, rivulets running back to the fathomless sea.

My aunts texted me asking if I had seen the inflation rate in Turkey. Before I could pull it up, they called me together.

"You wouldn't believe the cost," they said. I'd known it was high, high enough to rip the country open by its belly to starve and spoil. The last time I was in Istanbul a US dollar got you two lira. Now the articles reported twenty-five lira to the dollar. The police had been raiding onion and tomato warehouses accused of stockpiling. "Cheese by the slice," said one aunt. "Wrapped up in those little Styrofoam trays," chimed the other. "Say, you haven't got a small bundle of euros, have you?" they asked me.

I felt the sting of my own hunger, my face hot with shame. I had a few thousand euros sitting in the bank but no more coming in anytime soon. What could I say?

"It's your uncle," they explained.

He owned a plastics company, which had been fairly profitable for most of my life but was now on the brink of collapse. Just before the pandemic he'd purchased a new set of machines; I don't know what they did, but they cost millions of dollars each. Then the shutdowns hit and he bled money while the factory sat dormant. Things weren't closed long in Turkey, but long enough for him to hurt under the weight of his debt. If he'd purchased the machines from a Turkish supplier, if the loan had been in lira, inflation would've saved him. Suddenly seven million lira wasn't much more than the price of a little flat in Kuştepe. But his loan was in dollars, and his revenue was in lira. He'd be ruined in less than a year. "He's being optimistic—the rates . . ." my aunts said. "Haven't you got a little cash? You can't imagine what it would do."

That spring there would be another election. Erdoğan was running once more. He had been the president since 2014, and prime minister for more than a decade before that. A disastrous referendum had since dissolved the office of prime minister, making the president the head of the government too, on top of the additional executive powers Erdoğan had claimed in response to the failed 2016 coup. Though there were theoretically term limits, in effect there was nothing preventing him from a perpetual presidency. We were so far past the fig leaf of legal loopholes that Turkish corruption used to rely on—impressive, creative technicalities—now the government was practically advertising its abuse of power. The disrespect of not even caring enough to fool us! It seemed to be going the same way everywhere. You used to be able to expect a level of inventiveness from an authoritarian regime, but we'd grown tired. Look at us Turks, look at the Russians, the Hungarians, the Poles—we couldn't even be bothered to hold our tyrants to account.

I asked my aunts if they knew who they were voting for. It wasn't just the presidency that was on the ballot but all six hundred parliamentary seats. The opposition parties had been orchestrating a precarious coalition in recent months. The Council of Six, as they called themselves, was an odd assortment of secular nationalists, liberal conservatives, religious pro-Europeanists, socialist Kurds, environmentalists, and communists. It was a sordid mot-ley of Erdoğan's blustering political rivals without a single champion of the people in their ranks. There was still a lot of debate over who the candidate would be for this multi-party alliance, but most assumed old Kemal Kılıçdaroğlu, longtime head of the main opposition party, would be the challenger. He wasn't a particularly bad candidate, but he'd been running against Erdoğan for two decades, and nothing had ever come of it.

My aunts replied: "Of course, of course, whoever is there that isn't Erdoğan." I told them they had to care about their ministers too. Had they investigated candi-dates for next year's local elections? "Ah, you know so much. You know so much even though you're not here. Well here we are, and I don't know any of the candidates. I don't know any of the news stories you keep talking about."

"You must," I said.

"Oh no. It's too much. Let us know what you think when you look into it. Just let us know. But look here, have you got a few extra lira? Your uncle . . . us too . . . there isn't much to be done, I suppose," they said. They left a gaping silence after their comment, hoping I would fill it with offers of a few lira here and there, a monthly check perhaps to help, but instead I added only my own silence to theirs.

We said our goodbyes, and wished everyone in the world was happy and sent all the love we could muster to every end of the earth we could imagine. Putting down the phone, I felt strangely buoyant. My aunts had never seemed so helpless in their lives. The women in my family were generally hard-faced, well suited to adversity, and not especially political. We enjoyed bickering and haggling, holding grudges and committing small betrayals. We enjoyed being loud, obnoxiously loud, boisterously laughing and getting into shouting matches. We felt perpetually wronged and we liked that too, enjoyed a bit of guilt extracted from those around us, but we did not wallow. We provided for those in our lives. My aunts especially were quick to work extra hours and pick up odd jobs—in my childhood, when they were much poorer, the economy in shambles then too, they had even worked a few days a week as cleaners.

But their working days were behind them. Now they were decrepit. The older one had moved in with the younger one, renting out her own flat to save some money, but also to look after her sister, whose back was in bad shape. She'd been in a car accident in her thirties and had never fully recovered. Her spine was like this: gnawing, biting pain on the bad days, staticky on the good days. She needed rides to endless medical appointments. She couldn't carry grocery bags up to the apartment. Standing at the stove was a chore. They didn't tell me outright, but it was obvious that osteoporosis was setting in, hollowing out the bones of her right leg, hip, lower back. Her voice on the phone sounded dusty almost to match this (I must've imagined it, must've associated it with her), and every time I hung up it seemed as though fine sand was washing through my receiver and over my earlobe, down my neck. Her older sister was hardly more fit, her wrist and hand paralyzed by arthritis. Only on the wet days, she said, but in Istanbul there are only wet days. She did all the shopping, the driving; she harassed the doorman about repairs needed in the building; she called the bank about interest rates and family to ask for money for my uncle's failing business. She was wincing through life now—only on wet days, with those wet eyes leaking from the sting of arthritis. Sand and streams were the images fluttering in my head whenever my aunts called now. They were now desperate creatures, defined by a kind of erosion, and though this should have devastated me, though I did feel angry, I also felt more hopeful than I had in a decade. I was positively effervescent with hope. The country needed desperation, it needed resentment and rage, to shake it out of its fatal apathy. I knew my aunts were not alone in their suffering and I could see that suffering pushing them, reluctantly, toward some moment of action. I saw it bubbling up across Turkey, in the pundits' commentary, in the opinion polls, even in the tongue-in-cheek liquor advertisements that were going viral—this impending promise, this sense of hope that at last Erdoğan's grip might loosen, and breath would fill the lungs of millions, breath as the vise was released.

There were women in all the cells now. It was full, full to the brim, the prison, and it was getting fuller. Somehow it felt like there were, each night, a few more women sneaked into the prison when we weren't looking. They hadn't started doubling us up yet. Maybe there were more cells than they knew what to do with. Every woman they brought in was a step toward capacity, and then what, would they put a girl in my cell? An awful inner jump of excitement—a cellmate. But what would I do with her? How would I explain myself: my things, my clothes and food, the door?

I started hiding a few of the more glaring incongruities behind the toilet partition: the lounge chair, the lamp, the appliances and tea set. I kept the extra duvet and the books out in the open, in part because I didn't have room to hide them but also because I figured someone walking down a long row of cells wouldn't notice in a quick leap of the eye a bit of bedding or a few too many books. I thought I might paint a mural of my cell as it was supposed to look on some drywall, and set that up against the bars, but I didn't have paint, or artistic talent, or drywall, nor did I think it would fool anyone over the age of three.

My new habit of waking up in the cell made it more difficult to dodge the guards as they came by to let out the prisoners for exercise. I had started setting an alarm for each morning's recreation period so that I could jump out of my cot and back to Italy, but recently I was so tired I had slept through it more than once, rousing only moments before the guard reached my cell. One morning I was lazily still tucked up in bed when the lock clicked, and the door cracked open for the first time, giving me a startling look past my door, the hallway beyond the guard. I stayed put, shaking under my covers with my snout poked out, gesturing vaguely to the guard in a way that meant: *I'm fine, thank you, I think I'll stay here*, all while trying to steal a fuller peek outside my cell. He moved off without a word. A few days later, it happened again. I waved my little wave but the guard opened the cell door wider and folded his arms. It was time to get up and move.

"Oh no, really, I might be sick, I think."

"It's not a negotiation," he said.

I laughed, which he did not like, but I couldn't help it, or else I would've started shaking. I got up slowly from my cot, hoping he might move on to rouse the next woman, but he waited, no doubt skeptical, so I decided it would be better not to draw things out, swaddled as I was in a conspicuous duvet, surrounded by knickknacks that did not belong. I stepped into my slippers and staggered toward the cell door, almost blind with the shock of it. I hadn't ever really considered that I could leave—I thought I might fizzle and disappear as I crossed the boundary, like the things from the cell that I brought back into my flat. I stepped into the hall slowly, but the guard grabbed my arm and yanked me into the thin stream of women headed for the exit. He slammed my door shut after me. I heard myself making a pathetic giggling sound, not really laughter but a fluttering, panicked noise. There was a locked door between me and my bathroom, my flat, my father, Italy. I was trapped.

I jumped at the loud metallic clangs of other doors slamming down the row. The walls of the hallway were close, very close together, much closer than they had seemed from the safety of my cell, and the other cells were all packed neatly into their row—how narrow they looked from this side! Outside them slouched the figures of a dozen or so women, plodding toward the end of the hall, and I numbly copied them, shuffling over the concrete floor in my house slippers, the shushing sound discordant with the soft padded thumps of the inmates' footsteps. I kicked them off and regretted it at once, but what could I do? Each step made me more aware of the things that marked me out from the group: my wedding ring, the cell phone in my trousers that could ring at any moment, and beside it a half-empty sheet of ibuprofen tablets, which rattled very faintly as I walked, the unused tea bag in its paper envelope tucked into the breast pocket of my shirt. The Italian tags on my clothes. Turkish prisoners didn't wear jumpsuits, that was something, but I wouldn't withstand a close inspection. I wanted to strip then and there to remove all signs of my foreignness, to obliterate any hint that I might not belong. Instead, all I could manage was to untie my hair and let it fall over my face, hiding it uselessly from the glances of the guards.

I walked the long hallway with half of the other inmates, who, though a little surprised to see me, didn't make a fuss—to them I was just another new woman with a horror-stricken face. These guards looked different from the ones I had seen through the bars of my door. Their faces were grimmer, their expressions more accustomed to wounding. They led us down the long corridor to an intersection, then down an even longer corridor, and another—left, right, left, right, until up ahead a steady metal clang was echoing, growing louder as we approached. We were marched down a flight of stairs, then another flight, the temperature dropping as we reached the ground floor. I couldn't see over the women in front of me. I looked back. I couldn't see a guard for all the women behind me. I thought to slip away or to squeeze myself into a niche or doorway in the hall, but even if I could escape the group, I doubted I could find my way back to my cell.

We passed through another intersection of corridors and were flung out a set of heavy exterior doors into a freezing yard shaded from the low winter sun. There was no fence, or barbed wire, just four walls maybe ten meters high. I realized we were in a courtyard made of flanks of the prison wings. It was small, very small, and bare. On one wall was a door and a pair of windows with a darkened room behind them, on the other side was one large mirrored pane. There were other women already milling around the space, and I faltered and froze as my neighbors dispersed into the crowd.

In no time I was shivering so hard that, without thinking, I blurted out to the five or six nearby girls that I needed a coat, wouldn't the guards bring a coat? They stared blankly at me for a moment before one of them shrugged and turned away. None of them recognized my voice from my nightly pestering. None of them seemed to remember me from the day they were brought in, though I'd hounded each of them in turn for a bit of chitchat about Turkey—not the Turkey in the papers or on the lips of diplomats and politicians, but the Turkey of florists, taxi drivers, doorkeepers, miners, garbage collectors.

I was so nervous I could scarcely hear the world around me, my own thoughts pounding in my ears, and I decided to concentrate on counting the seconds, counting up and up, keeping time, not thinking about where I was but methodically stacking up the seconds, counting each moment, each dissected fraction of a moment until the recreation period would end and we would be herded back to our wing, and with no one to stop me I would sprint back to my cell, grip the bars of the door until a guard came and opened it for me, and I would at last be safe again, back in Italy. I was a fraud. I was conniving and self-serving and hypocritical but I didn't care so long as I could get back to the cell. If I could get back home, I could learn to live with myself.

After a few minutes, the guards opened a second door on the far side of the yard and most of the women started bustling toward it immediately. A rudimentary library, it turned out, with a few tables and chairs, not warm but warmer than outside—and in spite of my terror I was grateful for the shelter, my clothes were even less suitable for the weather than the other inmates'. I noticed that four or five women stayed outside, pacing in the yard, describing its circumference in a slow shuffle the way only people who have accustomed themselves to narrow lives can. Inside, the women seemed to be defrosting slowly, stamping their feet and grunting a few words to one another. I concentrated on the hum of the climate control and the shuffling sounds of their bodies. The women huddled at the five or six tables, hunching over a shared book and whispering a few things while turning the pages, so different from their chatty selves in our cells out of earshot from the guards, the supervisors, the warden. I sat apart, and from time to time I sensed their eyes on me. I recognized some of their faces from when they were brought in, but I couldn't tell whether they knew who I was. I told myself they had no way of knowing: they would assume I was just a new inmate. Besides, everyone was looking at everyone. You don't get to see a face for twenty-three hours a day, then suddenly there are fifty faces in an hour and you eat them with your eyes.

At last, a buzzer sounded overhead and the guards starting corralling everyone back into the main building. Walking back toward the cells, I felt deflated, ruined in a way I had no faculty to name. One of the women I vaguely recognized said: "See you tomorrow," in the offhanded manner of a joke. She said it to me, but also through me to the other women in the corridor and to no one at all. I sat on my bed and heard the guards walking down the row, locking each room in turn. Already they were taking out the next set of women. Yes, the woman said *See you tomorrow* the way everyone says it—meaninglessly—but now I was stranded in tomorrow, she was expecting to see me, and I would have to be there, ready when the guards came again to pull the women out of their cells and march them to the yard. I would be there with them, inextricably. And so did I have an obligation to be in my cell all the other times too, now that I was known, not only to be retrieved from it for recreation, but to be heard eating my meals, to be heard praying or singing or crying or cursing or sleeping? It was impossible for me to dedicate myself to this ruse day and night! I had a father who needed tending like a capricious flower! And what would happen if one day my neighbor was feeling friendly, and called out from her cell: "Hey, you who's always talking, you with the long hair, where are you from then?" and I was not there to reply?

I went into town, bought a tape recorder, and spent the rest of the day noisily living in my cell: getting up from the creaky cot and sitting down hard again; sighing a lot, muttering to myself; then for two hours or so I pretended to snore. It hurt my nose. By the end my mouth was all sandpaper, but I had a recording that I could put on whenever I wasn't home, which is to say, whenever I was home with my father instead of with the women in the prison.

As they kept taking us out for recreation, I thought I recognized one of the women in the library as the young girl who had cried herself to sleep. I'd only had a quick look at her when they brought her in. Now she was loitering by the bookshelves. The table behind her was empty. Most of the other women sat around the table near the exit. I went over to her and said excuse me and reached past her for a book, hoping to hear her voice, but she merely sidestepped me and turned toward the shelves. She looked like a prisoner in her own body, completely unaware or unacknowledging of her surroundings, and briefly I was filled with a sense of impending horror.

I flopped into a seat and made a lot of noise opening and turning the pages of the atlas I had grabbed. Just like when I worked in the schools, I made my presence obvious but not domineering—you had to let them talk first.

I huffed, and said a few *ah*s, then put the book back and calmly chose another from the same shelf and repeated the process. Finally, she sat down beside me though with her body still turned to the shelves. I met her eyes for a moment and smiled, then went back to reading my atlases.

"It's just pictures in there, or what?"

"Pictures, and some tables. Maybe I'll switch." I went to the biographies and grabbed one about Atatürk.

"You like reading?" she asked. It was her; I could tell— the same accent.

"Very much."

"You're the one with a cell full of books?"

I nodded. "Are we neighbors?"

She faced me in her chair now and nodded. She asked how I had so many books, if I had a relative who brought them for me, and then, almost inaudibly, if I could loan her one. She wasn't much of a reader, she said. She only liked the entertaining stuff, with spies, car chases, shoot-outs, gorgeous men and fatal women. "This library doesn't have any of that."

I told her my books were mostly people sitting around and thinking about things.

"Like you."

"I guess," I said.

"I'm bored enough to read anything."

"You'll return them?" I asked.

"I'm not going anywhere."

I nodded. "What's your name?"

"Müge," she said. I told her my name even though she

hadn't asked, but she didn't look like she heard me. She was watching out the window at the guards collecting the women from the yard. It was time to go home.

The next recreation period, having almost forgotten my promise, I grabbed the nearest book on my way out to the common area (a Turkish translation of Sartre's *The Wall*—truly a horrible little book, absolutely worthless in the best of circumstances, and certainly detrimental to someone in prison), and I felt a bit guilty for not having given her a bit more consideration. She took it cautiously, slinking back a few steps before reading the title.

"I've got three walls in my cell."

"This makes a fourth," I said, because I have a bad sense of humor.

After a few days she brought the book back and said she'd like something else if I had it, something more up-beat. I almost laughed. That's what my friends in Istanbul were always saying to me as well: "Dilara, don't you like to be happy? These novels are postured and depressing!" As much as my friends brightened up my days with their companionship, I wondered sometimes if they didn't find me a little too melancholic, if my moods weren't a burden to the friendships. They were frivolous characters, great patrons of white cafés and bright ice cream shops, and I suspected they hadn't thought of me in years. They never called.

That afternoon I went to the bookshop in town to buy Müge a stack of American detective novels. Proud of my generosity, I realized only after I got home that they were all Italian translations and therefore useless. No matter—

after dinner I ordered some Turkish translations from the internet and when they arrived the next week, I took them straight to my cell ready for recreation period.

"I thought you only had sitting-around-thinking novels," the young woman said when I next saw her, trying to sound put out, but she was a bad actor. I didn't have time to say *you're welcome* before she took them, smiling, under her arm.

After that she seemed to take more of an interest in me. We'd meet up in the library whenever we were on the same exercise shift. She began asking me about myself, and I was flattered, though I told her very little, only that I lived in Italy.

"When was that?"

"Just this morning," I said, seeing how much I could get away with.

"Yes, yes. I myself feel like I was in my parents' house just this morning as well—eating white cheese and sucuk. Then I woke up, I'm afraid."

She asked me where in Italy had I traveled and why I had moved back to Turkey, where in Turkey did my family call home, had I moved back for them? I told her what I could without putting my situation at risk, but every so often, I revealed one extra detail I shouldn't have. I felt guilty playing a trick, but everything was brimming with excitement for it. Who is this mischiever? Eventually Müge seemed satisfied, and she let me ask her about her own origins, if she was from Urfa or a hamlet in the east or maybe a suburb of Antalya. I asked her if she had siblings, children, parents.

"You have a lovely accent," I told her.

"The east. It sticks in the teeth."

"No. Some can sound sticky and harsh, some thick accents to my Istanbul ears, but yours sounds like a typewriter."

"Exactly," she said right away.

"No, no, my father—he always sounded like a type-writer to me. He was on them all the time. I enjoy the patter of it, like rain."

When I was in the cell, I didn't hate my father; he was removed from me, restored to that respectable distance of love. I thought that's what love was in families: it was an orbit. Whereas consuming or erotic love was always a collision, an obliteration of the distinct selves into a new, coupled whole, other kinds of love naturally remained on the periphery of our lives. I don't like this word *periphery*, because it discounts the completeness of love you feel for siblings, parents, cousins, so perhaps it is a question of motion, patterns. A healthy family has a relationship of tides, allowing some withholding, some concealment. There were no tides for me and my father anymore and no things hidden away—by the very nature of our constant presence in the other's life. Even with his mind slipping, even on the days when I was a stranger to him, I was a stranger plus. I was a stranger with connotations. I was a shroud in the shape of his past. I knew this grated against him. So I retreated to the prison, where I didn't have a shaky stomach from nerves, where I didn't rattle with anxiety about my father, my husband, the flat, the bank account, the medications clattering in my ears until I was deaf with grief.

I waited for dinner, passing the time like the other women: staring at the bars and trying not to fall apart. It was delivered every evening to the cell. Other prisons must have had cafeterias or messes or whatever they're called, but ours was a high-security wing, so all our meals were passed through a slot in the door. I had started taking these meals directly to my father to lighten the economic burden of cooking for two. I trusted the prison to provide.

I unpacked more and more of the storage boxes, boxes I didn't remember bringing into the cell, full of things I had not seen in years—one box was full up with bottles of Uludağ lemonade; another had the pressure cooker my grandmother used to make dolma. Or I stood in the center of the cell, concentrating hard on an object, and spun around slowly, turning to find it waiting for me: a newspaper from the stand at the head of my street, a parking ticket stub, a perfectly seasoned kebab, sometimes more abstract things like the stinging smell of the spice market, the song of a giddy muezzin, the bracing Meltem winds off the sea . . . I could spin one, two, three times, gorging on the city.

One morning I found Müge at our table in the library and immediately I could see something was troubling her. She looked almost ill, flipping through a book on decluttering your home without glancing at the pages. I asked her what was wrong.

"I am in love," she confessed.

He was from her village, a man who had also been arrested. She'd just received a letter from his brother; he'd been picked up by police last week and was now in Sincan Prison. She couldn't hold it in anymore, she said. "Who do I have to talk with about it? I have only been able to think: *If I ever get out, if I ever get out, I will run away with him*, now I have to hope he will ever be let out as well. I'm in love, sister, and it hurts."

She put me in mind again of my girlfriends in Istanbul. They were so quick to fall in love with a handsome devil at work, or even an actor they caught sight of outside a Starbucks. They made their lives into melodramas to match the soap operas they so preferred to the novels I recommended them. It was an odd rhyme, though, between Müge and my friends—her life was dramatic, genuinely troubled, while theirs were frivolous and borderline fictional. And perhaps my life was no less dramatic than hers—I was separated from my husband, did not know if he was safe, or when I would see him again.

I said to Müge that when she is let out, he too will be let out, maybe even before her. Things will eventually go right back to how they were. "You'll be able to pick up your life right where you left it," I said, trying to convince myself as well.

"And in the meanwhile? He's a good man, but prison, how could he survive it?"

I reminded her that she was surviving prison. I put my hand over hers and thumbed the ridge of her knuckles. "Why don't you have his family send you something of his, a book or a shirt. Your parents could send him something of yours as well, maybe."

"Oh no! My parents don't know anything about him. It's not what you think. I'm not deceiving them. I'm just a different person with them. It's easy for me to have separate lives. And now there is prison Müge."

Her comment tickled me, but it also made me sentimental, and I found I loved her for it. And it was true for all the women here, of course it was—such a simple but striking realization, that each of them had two lives, both inside the prison and out, just as vivid and fully wrought as my own—in fact, compared to me they were twice alive, whereas I was the same person in here as I was in my flat in Italy. Somewhere outside these cells they lived and loved and hurt and died and harmed the world, and were loved and harmed in return. I felt I was absolutely in love then— with Müge and with all the women. How easy it was! But I was always prone to this. If I had to explain it, I'd stumble for the right words. There aren't any right words—they don't exist yet.

I heard my mother's voice. I was sleeping, but where? My bed? The cot? It took some time to climb out of this dream, like climbing, hampered by sunscreen-slicked hands, up a slippery sea ladder. Blinking, I saw I was in the prison, the hallway buzzing with the harried snores of women, my own tape recorder buzzing with mine.

"Shh!" someone whispered to me.

"I'm sorry," I said.

187

Whoever it was spoke with a low voice, so low I couldn't understand them, just a gurgle of words like a lullaby.

"Who is singing?' I asked.

"Shh!" she whispered again. "There's no one here but the jinn playing cards."

"It's cold," I said, saying nothing to avoid saying anything.

"Quiet, quiet. You're tired. Off to sleep."

It was the voice of my mother—that phrase was always how she nudged me off to my bedroom.

"I can't sleep now," I told her.

Then for a moment it was Zeynep's voice replying through the wall, saying that there is always a little room for sleep in us, a little corner of ourselves where we can rest. I sat up and saw Zeynep's face now, that wide face, gazing through the cell bars at me. She told me there was time for worrying tomorrow, but it wasn't her voice, it was my mother's voice coming out of Zeynep's mouth. All down the hall, as women and girls stirred awake, the voice of my mother filled their mouths with reassuring hushes: "Off, off to sleep." I stood up from my cot and the women continued as if they could see me: "You need your rest, don't you want to grow big muscles?"

"I can't sleep," I said.

"Come, my darling, show us your muscles, eh?" my mother said from somewhere just beyond the cell door, and though I was alone, I could feel her take my thin arm between her thumb and forefinger, in a teasing pinch.

"I miss you," my mother said from the root of my own tongue. "I miss you and I can't sleep," said my mother with my lips and my teeth, her voice in my throat real as real.

I spun around to catch her standing there at the door of my cell, to catch her unlocking it and leading me down the hall and out into the city, but I wasn't fast enough, and there were only the dim bars of light on the floor, cast by the exit sign at the far end of the hall.

The voices stopped and the prison was silent with the thrumming of bodies in their sleep throes. I crept behind the partition, and my hand was on the doorknob when my feet skidded over two little rectangles on the floor, like flotsam washed onto the shore. They were the photographs of my family at the terrace restaurant. I couldn't believe it: for one thing, the camera that had taken the pictures was digital, not analog, and I had never had them printed— like all amateur photographers gifted a little camera on a birthday, I never got around to developing any of them, leaving them to languish on a hard drive. But these were glossy three-by-fives, clearly printed from proper film negatives, the kind you used to get from the one-hour photo center at the back of the pharmacist. I held them up to my face in the half darkness. They were almost exactly like the two I had found on the hard drive, but here was my mother in the first picture, sitting at the table. Her head back, slightly accentuating her slim neck and the taut rope of muscle down the side of it, her eyes closed in a smile, her one hand crooked in front of her with a water goblet coming to her lips and the other draped over the back of my father's chair. It was an impossible picture, she was dead these days, ten or twelve years dead at the time of the pictures, yet here it was, a perfect facsimile of the original, as reliable as drowning.

I walked slowly back into the flat, opening my laptop to compare the images. They were the same, exactly the same, in all the details I had misremembered, differing only, starkly, by the presence of my mother in one version. I stared at the picture and its double, studying how closely I resembled my mother, delighting especially in the weird closeness of our apparent ages in the picture. Engrossed, I missed entirely my father getting up to pee, then roving through the flat for a while, and finally returning to his room. In the morning, I woke up blind with all the lights on. My laptop was bent open under my arm. The two glossy prints were on the nightstand. I showered in a trance and was about to go wake my father when I caught a glimpse of the photos on the nightstand that pricked me with worry. They were changed now—exact copies of the digital ones, busy, the colors a little dull, too many faces, the anonymous inlet, and no trace of my mother, her void exactly where it should be.

I wondered if I never wanted children because my mother died so young, as if having a kid of my own might somehow number my days. Being myself childless, my memories of my own youth had become like offspring—what a silly image! My husband used to say I was a hypocrite, laughing that I didn't want kids but worked in child development. I hadn't really expected to become a psychologist—I'd been fascinated with psychology, yes, but my father insisted I train in psychiatry. He and his political science colleagues ridiculed their own psych students. There was money in it, I said, but no matter how rational my argument, I couldn't convince him I wasn't suited for medical school—not until I told him that I thought Mom would've wanted me to work with children.

I wasn't committed against having my own children. If I'd been pressured by a more domineering husband—well, I'd never much thought about it. I didn't have to; my husband only ever wanted kids for what he called the wrong reasons: something to brag about if they favorably resembled you and also a guaranteed caretaker as we aged. He stopped mentioning the latter after we took my father in. It was for the best, we didn't have time, and neither of us could bear the idea of all the effort. Besides, I couldn't imagine what I'd have done about childcare now, in this predicament, and with no mother of my own to guide me through motherhood.

I had never known my mother as another adult, as a person, so I missed her only childishly. Some children, whether because of estrangement or loss, never discover the personhood of their parents, something that can happen only when you become a person yourself, when you face the bracing air of growing up. I often wondered what she would say to me now, but I had only the dialogue of childhood in her mouth: *Quiet, quiet. You're tired. Off to sleep*; *Food isn't just chocolates and pastries, Dilara*; *Bedtime has arrived in a wonderful sports car.* These phrases were useless in the face of my father's illness. What would she have done to help him?

It hurt all the more as I came to realize that—the way his memory was working, the way he sometimes conflated her and me, and forgot altogether her death—he still had a wife, alive and buzzing in her kindness, but I had only grasping memories of a mother. This bile of resentment lurched up my throat.

Sometimes, filled with a craving for deceit, I actually leaned into these delusions. When he called me Ayşe, I didn't correct him. Instead, I had taken up the strange task of talking about myself in the third person, in part because I never heard my own name otherwise now that my husband was gone, but also because it often prompted my father to mistake me for my mother.

Worrisome, I knew, for a daughter to torture her father this way—a trick that better belonged in an ancient tragedy than in the furtive acts of malice between caregiver and care receiver—but consider this: it was a mercy too, because he believed it. So convincing was my father's whiplash return to the past, it momentarily tricked me into believing that nothing bad had ever happened, that my youth, still unspooling, was just beyond the window out of which he spent his days staring.

"Ayşe," my father would call. "Will you, will you . . . Ayşe!"

I'd come back into the flat. The lights would be out everywhere and the late afternoon sun would drown us in heavy daylight, heavy shadows.

"Yes?"

"Ayşe . . . please . . ."

It was easy for me to pretend to be my mother. She had

a few mannerisms I could mimic, having grown up watching them as all children scrupulously watch their parents in domestic performances: pulling a brush through her hair before her mirror; lighting a thin stick of incense, having just finished mopping the floors; flicking a bit of thread between her tongue and lip before starting up her needlework.

In my father's reality, my mother had never died and his country had never betrayed him. How marvelous for him to have shed these truths. Guilt had begun to corrode me as my father wriggled about in his final stage of death—guilt because dementia is so crippling and destructive that, in order to protect yourself, you build distance between it and you, between yourself and your parent who is forgetting you. Guilt because as he shouted, or crashed a family heirloom to the floor, or vomited all over himself and the couch and the carpet, the only sane thing to do was get upset. I felt the rage curling inside me. I cursed him often. I cursed him for reducing us both to this horrible state in which he was infantile, idiotic, spasmodic as a toddler, this man who had always represented wisdom and refinement, this man who had raged against dictators, against oppressors, against fanatics of cruelty, and yet here he was now—insignificant, sputtering, beyond help. It was this every day; I hated him and then myself for hating him in the first place. I pitied him and then myself together. Some days I owed him the world, as every child owes a parent, and other days I owed him nothing, just as every child owes a parent. He couldn't help any of it, and I couldn't help him with any of it, so it was easy then, almost an apology, to put on the perfume my mother used to wear, and hum as she had while I filled the kettle, and hum as it boiled, and hum as I poured generous servings of milk and sugar into my father's tea and brought it to him. I put on some music, Mahler, that my mother had listened to while she puttered through her mornings. I turned my father's chair to face the window, to catch not the point of the sunset, but its falling blades—blue, blue, white, yellow, orange, purple, dusk. I told him I loved him and left him there with his tea. He seemed peaceful, but that might have been my optimism reading the stillness of his face and refusing to see that he was gone—hundreds of meters, dozens of years, stretched, pulled, and eventually squeezed out of reality and forced edgewise into a desolate, if pacific, history of the self. His hallucinations were as real to him as anything. The picture show of his brain did what it could to keep up a few flickering images of light, a bit of narrative, our great addiction. I helped where I was able. I tried to give him a pleasant hour here and there before he forgot not just my mother's death, but her altogether.

In time I began to provoke my father's misrecognition more actively. I'd go about my own chores, vacuuming and mopping the floors, wiping down the stove and counters, scrubbing the shower and toilet, and I'd say: "Oh, Dilara doesn't ever pick up after herself"; "Dilara has made a mess of the kitchen again"; "What shall we do with little Dilara?" I couldn't look at him and do this, it felt too deceitful. I knew these were no longer just trickster performances for my father but the preoccupations of some baser need in me. I'd spend the day imagining that a younger, smaller version of myself had wrecked through the house, and it was like I was building my mother out of these phrases, these actions. Soon enough she was in the hallway, humming and picking up discarded socks. And when my father looked at me, thinking I was her, I could see the trove of his love, I could see his hunger—he recognized me again even if it wasn't me that he recognized. I don't know, it was better than being mistaken for a stranger. He looked at me and saw a face that he loved, and I fell to pieces.

I gave Müge books, yes, but then I brought her also a little square of bitter dark chocolate, which she ate hungrily, though she admitted it was not her favorite. So it became a game of guessing her favorite sweet: next was marzipan, then caramel, then licorice, then Italian nougat—all the while she never told me which she preferred, but she ate each of them with such haste it was as if there would never be a day without candy. I was pleased to be able to provide a bit of happiness for someone. Müge didn't ask me how I was getting her sweets. Instead, she asked harmless things about myself: Did I have any siblings, any children, any spouse? What had I done for work? Did I think about the first meal I'd cook when I got out? What was my name, again?

"I'm sorry. You've been so kind. It's embarrassing. I forgot it as soon as you said it."

I told her it was Ayşe.

Why did I lie? Maybe it was a way to protect myself—to

avoid the dangerous truth? I found myself answering all her questions as if I were my mother. I had a husband, yes, and a daughter. My husband was unwell, my daughter was a psychologist. I had lived in Ortaköy all my life and was a devoted housewife.

We talked until the guards deposited us once more into our cells, and then when they left, we continued talking. The hall was like a whisper gallery, the strange acoustics linking cells, and sometimes you would get other girls' comments like changing the radio. We talked until the lights went out, and talked even beyond that— all the while, I answered everything just like I imagined my mother would have; all the while, I put on her affectations until Müge must've dozed off, and even then, I went on talking, talking as my mother until she answered me back from the walls of my cell. I wasn't doing her lines anymore—she was here before me, here with me. She laughed and all at once I forgot everything.

There was an urgent rapping at the front door of the flat, and I jumped back in from the cell to see Lucia letting herself in, with Giovanni following quickly behind. "We were worried about your father," said Lucia, marching toward the kitchen. "Gian told me he was dying of boredom, just the two of you here."

Giovanni set a large tote bag full of food on the kitchen counter with a wink: "I said *you* must be bored and could use some company around here."

Lucia carried on talking though I no longer listened as

she went through their bag, retrieving two bottles of wine that were immediately opened, several cheeses wrapped in paper, a link of salami, rosemary sprigs. From my cupboards she took out olive oil and pepper, mixing them with the rosemary in a dish, then she produced a cutting board and began slicing the salami into thick pads. Giovanni, moving in a way that was probably meant not to draw attention to himself, sidled out of the kitchen. I listened as he wandered from room to room (which did not take long in our flat), apparently checking for something, though I could only guess what.

"What are you two doing here?" I asked at last.

"Oh, poor Dilara, I couldn't stop thinking of you," said Lucia. "How you haven't got much of a life right now, I mean with your father here like he is—slowly getting better, I mean. And your husband having to work so far away and for how long, who knows? I thought to myself, *Dilara could use a little entertainment, a little checking in.* You know I think I was meant for checking in on people, isn't that right, Gian? I can always produce a spread of hors d'oeuvres at a moment's notice. I think sometimes I might be contracted by the national disaster relief bureau!"

I stepped into the hallway. Giovanni was at the end of it, peeking into my bedroom. A strange sensation, like the flat had been tilted at an angle and I was scraping across the face of the room. Had he gone through my apartment the other day when he was here alone with my father? I felt this terrifying chill swell the canals of my brain. Had he found the prison?

"Does your dad need help?" he asked over his shoulder,

without turning away from my room. I walked cautiously toward him.

"What are you looking for?" I replied.

Giovanni turned to face me. "Ah, there he is! How is the old man feeling today, like a conqueror?" With a quick arm at my shoulder, Giovanni turned me around and walked us both toward my father, who had just emerged from somewhere looking like an unearthed turnip. Giovanni jollied us all into the living room and pulled the tavla board out from under the coffee table, then set about straightening the throw pillows and blankets, and clearing the table of mugs and bowls, and pinning back the curtains to reveal the room to the days, the hours in their passing. Just as he disappeared into the kitchen with hands full of our domestic detritus, Lucia appeared with a tray of sweetmeats, cheeses, jams, breads, cured meats, relishes, and glasses of wine. In no time they had the flat changed into a respectable if not entirely welcoming home.

"Will your husband be back anytime soon?" asked Giovanni, settling himself cheerily in an armchair and popping an olive into his mouth. "A week or two more? He doesn't answer when I call him."

"I think he has a new number," I said. "But it's just me and Dad here for the foreseeable future."

"To leave you like this!" said Lucia, and I found myself thinking the same thing, that I was fed up.

I told Lucia she was right. "I'm afraid I don't have much of a life here."

"Oh, Dilara, I was only teasing. No reason to get sentimental. You have us, and your father, and you simply must come round to our place and help me cope with my cousins next week. Oh, and my nephew's christening— I could really use your advice on the china patterns . . ."

Slowly I relaxed a little, as it became clear that Giovanni was not going to confront me about the prison. He must have been looking for my husband, to see whether he had miraculously returned, or if not that, looking for signs that I was not mistreating my father, or at least that I was coping with him. I realized as Lucia went prattling on and Giovanni merely nodded beside her, insistently, reassuringly—the pair of them were worried, I think for me, yes, but also for my father, also for my husband. I took no comfort in this. Their interest felt accusatory—with my domestic life conspicuously spiraling out of control, how could it not?

"I just don't feel . . ." What was I trying to tell them? What did I want to say to them as, watching me, they pulled thick blobs of jam across warm slices of bread?

"Do you need anything? A bit of help, I mean?"

"Of course, Gian, of course she could use a little help, huh? Ah, I forgot, I had gotten you a little gift, I had forgotten your birthday. Well, I forgot the gift too, Gian, leave some money on the table, that will make up for it. Does your father have birthdays, too? Leave him some money as well. You both need a new pair of house slippers. Yes!"

"And I could stop by again tomorrow," said Giovanni. "Maybe take your father out to the café?"

Instantly I shook my head. I didn't want Gian prowling around the flat, bumping into my secret prison. But they wouldn't take no for an answer; they thought I was just being selfless, not accepting the help.

"I'm not at home," I told them at last.

"Well of course not," said Lucia. "No, this isn't your home. We know that, darling. Oh, you'll go back to Istanbul eventually, and we'll be depressed. Gian will have to stuff with me ice cream, I'll be brokenhearted at your departure, but you'll go back. Maybe soon. Things change so fast—politics, bawk, bawk, bawk, quick!" She snapped her brined fingers.

"Eventually, you'll go back to Istanbul," said Giovanni slowly. He wasn't looking at me, though; he was watching my father struggling to spear an olive with a toothpick. "And we can watch your father for a little while," he added quickly, as if realizing he should, for my benefit, pretend my father was immortal.

"Yes, yes! You could go back tomorrow and we'll come over to take very good care of your father. We'll come over either way. Didn't I say I was the best at checking in on others? Tea! Next time tea and finger sandwiches, the English way."

"You'll go back to Istanbul," said Giovanni, taking my father's hand and guiding the toothpick through the slippery flesh of the olive.

This morning, I was scrambling eggs, and distractedly thinking silly thoughts (it must be much more affordable to live in a prison cell than the same-sized studio apartment in this housing market), and thinking about what sorts of jobs I could get (post officer; pharmacy cashier; window washer), when my father started shouting. He was calling out as if to me, but he wasn't saying any names I recognized. I found him stripped naked save for his socks, sitting on the toilet with the door flung wide open. That must have been when the notion first struck me: because he had already mastered the art of publicly defecating, the best place for him would be the prison cell in my room. This thought sounded at first like a little joke with myself. It wasn't until after I'd helped him clean himself, led him back to his room, and laid out his clothes that my reaction coalesced into a clear notion that truly, the best place for someone like my father, the best place for someone without any memories, is a prison.

Or rather, the person best suited for a prison is one without any memories. They will get their meals. They'll get their medications. They don't have rent due or checks to remember to put in little envelopes and send to the utility companies. They can get air and exercise in the yard without getting lost. Minimum-security prisons were actually a step above hospice care: they were largely the same thing, with the same expectations of mistreatment, but the prisons were free.

Over the next few days, I grew this idea in me the way an oyster grows a pearl: the worst aspect of prison was the monotony; each small repetition stacking on the last, a cumulative bulk so massive that its gravity starts to blot out other aspects of oneself, of other, happier memories. That was the true torture—how it replaced you from the inside out with the impossible weight of monotony, until you lost the person you were before, you lost their joys and sorrows and hopes, and you became yourself a prison cell. Hollow yet heavy.

It was an especially cold day in the rec yard. Everyone was in the library; the tables were all full. I saw Müge for the first time in a few days and we huddled together on the floor, leaning against a bookcase. I passed her the last bit of caramel I had left. I felt I owed it to Müge to keep bringing her more sweets, more books—yes, but what did I owe my father? How many packets of oatmeal could I have bought him for the price of a fancy chocolate? I watched her inhale it, before she leaned over and rested her head on my shoulder. I smiled and asked her if she'd had enough sweets yet.

She shook her head. "My mother promised to send me some künefe, but she hasn't yet. When it arrives, you can have some too." The way she promised it, so earnestly and without hesitation, broke my heart.

I asked if she missed her family, and she admitted that she didn't much. She laughed then, a panicked jolt, and apologized to me as if she had offended all families. It was sickening, she said, to be around such sweeties, such dearies as her mother, her aunts, her father, her uncles, all of whom treated her with such care and affection, yet would go out into their lives with suspicious eyes, cynical intentions, distrust and cruelty their mainstays.

"They will vote for him again this year," she whispered to me.

"Maybe not," I said.

"Will you?" she asked, forgetting our situation, though most of the women had not yet been tried, let alone sentenced, so technically they still had the right to vote, if that counted for anything. "They donate to charities for the poor and then they go out and vote for a scoundrel, a con man who drapes his family in silk and power. They say it is pious to love the world and then they come home from the mosque, vile-tongued, saying we ought to hang ten refugees for every one caught committing a crime. My mother—you wouldn't believe—she worked hard, went to college, she runs her own business, and now she nods along to these stooges who say a woman is only a birthing vessel. So much anger, so much violence in their voices, and then they turn to me and say what a beauty, what a bright girl who shall conquer the world."

I wanted to interject, to tell her that not all parents are like that, sometimes they're the firebrands, the rebels, look at my father I almost said, but that wouldn't have been useful to her. I listened.

"I don't know, auntie; how can I say it? You grow up protected by these two golden beams of sunlight that are your parents and then finally you see them for what they are, harsh and crude lamps."

"They'll come around," I said. "They'll understand you eventually."

"They haven't even been here to visit me."

"It's a long trip from the east," I said.

Müge nodded. She toyed with the caramel wrapper. "Your family is more generous. Look at all the things they bring you. Look at all the books, the candy. I saw a tea kettle; how do you have electricity?"

I sat up straight.

"Don't worry, auntie. But how come this is the last caramel?"

I watched her turning the wrapper, twisting and untwisting its corners. I took it back from her and quickly hid it in my pocket.

My father was no longer interested in the television. I'd gone out of my way to stream Turkish soap operas for him, but he had eyes now only for the window in the living room. We lived too far inland for the sea to be visible, and even so, the mountainsides would've prevented it, as our flat was tucked squarely in a cleft between shallow, rocky hills. But my father looked out the window and saw a narrow strip of shore, scalding under the sun, full of glittering, crashing waves; he saw pearl divers coming up with their treasures; he saw gulls and domes and thin minarets. I saw only scruffy, fat hills, a long March sky still in the shadow of winter.

A man was walking in the street below with a spool of cable over one shoulder.

"Hey, fisherman!" my father shouted to him. "Hey, fisherman!"

The poor man looked and saw a deranged codger shouting incomprehensibly from his window.

"He's not a fisherman," I said.

"Hmm."

"That's not the sea."

"Hmm."

It didn't make sense to me, perhaps because I had my senses still, and I needed to lose them all to understand my father. I was looking with my eyes, hearing with my ears, but he was looking and listening with some other organ of sense. It was terrifying to watch a person disappear into some other reality and leave their body behind. I couldn't even watch people sleeping—I never liked watching my husband sleep. Some lovers did this, so the romances say, watched the other in their dream shivers. Watch and see the eyes shake. It was terrifying, like looking at a corpse before shrouding it for burial. It was the most revolting thing in the world to me: an empty body.

The phone rang and I told my father to keep it down at the window, where he kept shouting at the pitiful repairman.

"Have you bought a pet?" my husband asked on the other end.

"A pet?" I said.

"A pet to keep you company. Isn't that a nice way to ask whether you have replaced me yet, I mean."

"I did," I said, laughing. "But the Turkish special forces came down in a helicopter and took him, saying they were here to arrest my husband for crimes against the state."

"An effigy then?"

"That means it's safe to come home," I said.

"Please, please, please," he said slowly, slowly.

"I don't want to hear from you if you're not going to have a sense of humor," I said.

"You live in a fantasyland."

"Someone's got to face the fantasy. We can't all escape away into the harsh absurdity of life."

"Do you need any money?" He always asked this when he called. Each time this blush hot as color pooled at the nape of my neck. I had seen, from checking our bank account, that my husband had not spent a cent since his departure. "How are you surviving?" I asked.

"I can't explain," he said. I think he meant he was ashamed of whatever work he was doing, whatever lowly job would pay him in cash, whatever hostel would rent him a room cheaply, but it could also mean that somehow no one was taking any money from him, somehow he was going through the world completely on credit, and I smiled so hard at this because he was the kind of man to be troubled by it; he could never let a good thing happen to himself without crying.

"Are you punishing me?" he asked.

"I don't want to hear from you again," I said, the smile still on my face, though everything behind it was gone.

"I'll have a sense of humor."

"No. Regardless. I don't want to hear from you because I must move on now."

"If not from your father's death, you'll at least move on from me?"

How cutting, to be seen so brightly lit by someone so myopic, someone from whom I hoped still to have a few secrets. I hung up. Is my father dead? Not yet, not yet.

I told myself that there was no point in being hopeful.

I knew the outcome and it was not avoidable. There was absolutely nothing as certain in life as my father's deterioration and death. *Inevitable* didn't feel like a heavy enough word to capture the density of this grief. Each night before I fell asleep, before I could even begin to fall asleep, I promised myself: *It is happening tomorrow, my father will die tomorrow.* And then what did my mind do but immediately go against my wishes, thinking of the day after tomorrow, *What will I feed Dad for lunch?* I thought of him saying: *Thank you for the food, I really enjoy it.* How do you throw a net over your own mind, how do you trap it and pull it out from the sea of hope? I used to think it was good to be optimistic, to believe in things while maintaining a sort of educated pragmatism, but when there was nothing, nothing, nothing but guaranteed loss, guaranteed pain, what was that if not torture? And so why prolong it?

Hope is a symptom of the strangeness of life. Who was I to say what is and isn't possible while I hid a prison in my bathroom?

Our minds are built for pattern finding, consciously and unconsciously. So much in life follows patterns, rhythms, predictable responses or at least a limited number of possible scenarios, but life itself is not a pattern, and it shares this lesson with us every day, and we—so benighted in our obstinate need for sense, linearity—find patterns anyway, and we call this hope. It will kill you eventually. It will teach you in death that you have been fooled, tricked by yourself. This is what I said to myself as I lay awake at night, neurons firing helplessly toward a better life. What a torturous existence to have a bit of imagination.

Like the sea, silence has many faces. The kind covering over the prison this morning was somber; it had everyone's glances jumping into themselves. The guards too were swallowed under this quiet. You could feel it on the skin. You could feel it like a stone dribbling from the nape of your neck down the steps of your spine. It was the kind of silence that comes from being the only person in a room not in on a miserable joke. What can you do—ask for it to be repeated?

The guards brought us into the yard as normal but then they retreated back into the building and locked the doors behind them. They knew something and we sensed it—they couldn't face us, couldn't bear to be with us, in our state of not-knowing. All around me, the women's faces were shot through with nerves. I waited and waited for someone to speak, to crack the glass silence. Across the yard, a woman sobbed. I looked around for Zeynep; she would know. She shook her head as she told me, an accident in the east—huge—hundreds dead.

"A power plant," whispered Müge at my side. "Or a dam. There are dams all over my province." She added quickly as an afterthought and then she repeated, there was a dam upstream from her village.

"Or a mine collapse," guessed another woman, her voice bouncing out of her, too loud into the blank air around us.

Only halfway through the recreation hour, the guards returned us to our cells without letting out the other group. Back inside, speculations grew, echoing down the row. Someone said a state of emergency had been declared, another said there was a coup in the works, but tracing these rumors back down the line of cells turned them all to dust. The guards stayed up in their office, not even bothering to shout over the loudspeaker for us to keep quiet. I could feel their panic rising, frightened most of all by the things no one had said, by the guesses no one could bear to make, and I wondered whether they were thinking of all the life outside this prison, all the ill fortune, all the tragedies that were befalling their families, their friends, their pets, their houses, their neighborhoods. They traveled by fearful daydreams out of the prison, walking in fantasy under cold and heavy suns back to their homes now rubble, wailing at their families now rubble, while they remained trapped in this concrete palace aching for it to become rubble.

Then from far down the hall, maybe at the very end (though did the hall ever end? not from what I had seen), someone got hold of the truth, maybe the girl on the end had nicked it off a guard, and it traveled quickly between the cells in a lengthening chain of certainty: there had been an earthquake in Gaziantep, a city of two million. The row erupted in anxious chatter, each woman speaking all her fears over the others. The guards could no longer ignore us, and at last came through the hall, telling us to calm down, telling us not to rouse ourselves into a rabble. They came down the row in such measured steps (though

209

we could plainly see they too were anxious), speaking in calm, careful voices from those harsh faces, shell-shocked as they repeated the scant information they knew. They were saying the buildings were not up to code. They were saying it was a mess. The emergency services could only guess at the extent of it, because the cell towers were down, not a word in or out. You might as well throw a dart in the dark to get the numbers of dead and dying. The loudspeaker blared, calling the guards back to their office, but we pleaded with them to stay, as if they had answers tucked into their pockets. We hammered on our doors, wishing a guard would come back, until one at a time a man would run down the hallway, or shout from the exit an update.

The news trickled in across the rest of the day, grim updates announced periodically by a guard sent down the row. It was not just Gaziantep, but Maraş, and Göksün too. An enormous earthquake had hit in the thin morning hours: 7.8, tied for the most powerful earthquake to strike Turkey, the great tableland of fault lines. Thousands of aftershocks rippling through eastern Anatolia, then just after lunch a second earthquake. From Hatay on the coast all the way to Malatya, a corridor of earthquakes over three hundred kilometers long, hitting fives, sixes, and sevens on the Richter scale. The soil had liquefied, swallowed up buildings, shattered others, rent open whole cities under the gray February sky.

God, each woman, the shriek let out in turn when the name of her village was called out by a guard coming now and again with an update from their office. Screams mounted in the prison hall, in the cells, condensing, condensing, condensing with no place to escape—the pressure was insurmountable. All afternoon, all evening, the women cried the names of villages and cried for the beloved dead imprisoned in the earth a thousand kilometers away. I stayed up to hear the guards come back and tell us the search parties had been halted by the freezing weather, the speculation that the cold snap would seal the fates of thousands more stuck under the rubble. I stayed up listening, though I had no words of comfort. It would be enormous, the catastrophe, but no one talked that way yet, all the guesses were still conservative, all thoughts were on the rescue efforts. I stayed up until the morning, until I couldn't take it anymore. I went back to my flat in Italy.

Well, what did I expect out of tragedy? Exile is an abusive relationship, and even when you leave—when you pack up your duffel bag, and take off into the long, long sea hoping to resurface in some shining world without pain, and instead end up in a place with its own harms and passions and joys and tortures (that is everywhere), and you set up a life again, safeguarded this time, put into a special box—your homeland reaches out a cruel hand and injures you again, even here, even in your haven, because what people don't mention about exile is the hostages it creates. For every exile, there is a family of hostages, a host of lovers, friends, colleagues, rivals, affable greengrocers, lascivious taxi drivers—all left behind in their hostage's bindings, and the country calls out that it misses you, don't you miss it back? To prove it, it is time for pain! and it kills fifty thousand people, and your pain is no greater than that of those back home, it might even be a little less, shielded by distance, diluted by time spent adulterously in other lands, but the country wants its blood, wants to see you writhe, to remind you whence you've come, what soils your worm-ridden ancestors lie under. Have you become immune to your motherland? Its wounds against you don't bruise or scab over or scar—they itch and ache like a phantom limb. Each catastrophe cuts off another piece of the body—and is the mother country enacting these mutilations, or is the body itself performing them, some bloody act of self-preservation? National tragedies are national tragedies, but even the smallest horrors, the mundane misfortunes of existence, are enough to disappear little pieces of the self behind a numbing pain—loss, loss, loss becomes intangible, a void, and with each loss, eventually I will be gone.

I know a woman who fled Syria. She took up crochet, and lawn bowling, and tried to ride horses so she could play polo, and she went for a swim each morning and a long walk each evening and she made her children's clothes, and she taught herself the art of French pastry, and she read a book a week, and she wrote an essay on flamenco dancing, and she visited the graves of many philosophers as a sort of pilgrimage, and she took a train to Vienna, then Prague, then Munich, then Berlin, then Amsterdam, then Paris, then London, then New York, then Toronto, then Chicago, then Denver, then Los Angeles, then Hawaii, then Sydney, then Singapore, then Mumbai, then Cairo. She looked for Syria in all of them but never saw it again.

I did not go back into the prison for three weeks. I didn't even bother playing the tape recorder. I selfishly indulged in the separation from my country none of the other women could afford. They were in a grotesque limbo, trapped in the prison, unable to ignore reality but unable to scurry back to their towns and villages, to join the search missions, to pull any scrap of news about their loved ones out from the maelstrom of grief. I couldn't bear it, the peeling horror. I couldn't stand checking the news except to watch the cold numbers of the death toll climb and climb above every pundit's worst guesses. I was appalled, and yet I also felt some perverse hope for even greater disaster, I relished the emotional distress swelling inside me—it was as if I needed to prove I was Turkish. I wanted to feel the rising death toll as an exponential pain in myself, wanted to feel that I was hurt a hundred, a thousand, a million times over and still had hurt left. I needed to make sure I had not lost myself behind the curtain of exile. Why wrap my identity into this tragedy, into all the tragedies of the country? Shamelessly I immersed myself in disasters that didn't belong to me, but not just that—no, not just anyone's tragedies!—I wanted to wrap myself in the miseries of Turkey as some dysfunctional sense of identity, some fucked-up need to take part in sadness as a form of belonging.

I wanted to tell my father about all of this, but it wouldn't mean much to him. I wanted to shovel a bit of grief into his mouth, force it down his throat if only to give myself the company, but he was immune. What was he, anymore, my father? Hardly a person. He was the leftovers of a life.

"Get away," my father said. "Out, out."

I pulled the blanket off him and told him to stand up, to move, to give his legs a little use for the day.

"Fuck," he said. "Fuck you."

I took his arms in my hands and counted to three and lifted but he stayed stiff, as if each of his muscles had ossified. He refused to help me help him stand. I pulled and pulled and got him out of his chair.

"No. Fuck you. I'm not, I'm not . . . fuck you."

"What's the trouble?"

"I don't know."

"Why are you talking this way?" I asked.

"Because I don't like you."

"You don't know me," I said.

"That's not correct."

"Yes. I am nobody," I said.

"I can't stand you," he said. He meant it. When you spend enough time with someone slipping in and out of reality, you can almost sense their lucidity, you can feel when the words mean something. But you don't always guess right, and those miscalculations hurt the most—when they seem momentarily cogent, as if there isn't anything wrong with them, and only after the conversation has continued for several minutes do you stumble on the first clue that they're speaking to you from a different place, a different time. Suddenly, you realize you've followed them down into the undertow, swept up in the illusion of their clarity, and the whole time you have both been operating in a hallucination. You feel both duplicitous and a partner victim of the dementia, almost like you might become unstuck from reality yourself. Or are you unstuck already? Can you still get out or are you trapped in the delusion? They are the drowned and you are the drowning.

But right now, my father was not in that underwater place. He was entirely aware of me. I could tell. Maybe he couldn't see me for his daughter but he could see me. I had the sense, the way his intelligent eyes were turning, that he knew I looked like my mother but was not her, and this meant to him that she had died. My face was death—that was the knowledge behind him saying: "Fuck you, fuck you, fuck you."

I moved my father's cane. I always moved his cane. I'd trip over it because he'd leave it somewhere, these damn stand-on-their-own canes—they were black so they blended into almost every corner of the flat. I'd pick it up and put it right beside him, wherever he was, and maybe twenty minutes later, he moved and took it only part of the way with him and I'd trip on it again. I tripped on it now and I moved it, but I didn't say "Dad, here's your cane," and I didn't stand it right beside him. I put it behind him while he was fixing himself a cup of tea. Quietly even. I don't want to say I crept up behind him. Who knows what came over me. You ask one toddler why they hit another and they say they don't know. We don't believe them but we should. They don't know because they don't have the words to describe why they did something. I had tested a lot of kids over the years, and I always believed them when they said they didn't know why, they didn't know, and I tried to believe myself too.

I was in my bedroom when I heard him stumble and hit the floor hard. I wasn't sure but it sounded like he might have hit the counter too. I didn't get up. I stayed in my bed for a minute, then another minute, then a third, listening to these shallow and almost wet sounds, the sounds of old and rasping flesh—chicken cutlets over a nicked-up butcher block. My chest seized but I didn't run to my father—I couldn't. It hurt me and I deserved to hurt. I deserved to hurt for hating him, and I deserved better than all of this. I deserved better than a dying father, an absent husband, a squandered country. I am human and so I deserve. I would go to him and we would hurry to the emergency room, but right now I was trying to breathe.

PART V

THE DAYS WERE FOG. As much as I wished it would disappear, I couldn't keep away from the cell forever. When I eventually went back, its allure felt stronger than ever. When I couldn't be in there I stayed shut up in my bedroom just to be closer to the prison, like magnetism. Day and night, the irresponsibly few times I left my room to check on my father, give him his pills, or wash him in the tub, I found myself drifting back to the cell. I had begun staying up for consecutive nights, waiting in my cot for my mother to come around the cell's partition symmetrical to the way she used to poke her head out from around the corner of the kitchen as I sprawled belly-down in front of the television. Sure enough, here she was, with a chic floral scarf tied over her hair like Sophia Loren. She produced a tray of strong tea and honeycomb with cookies, and we fell at once into a long happiness. I drank and ate and squealed in conspiratorial excitement. Time stretched and large, wide windows opened up beside us. They filled the cell, and we were pressed, squeezed by sunlight in thick panes.

"Oh, here comes your father," my mother said. Now and then, as if to mark the end of our time together, my mother said: "Here comes your father, back from work at last!" whisking the tarpaulin dream away and leaving me submerged in the shallow light of the prison, my father just outside my room, screaming, screaming because he didn't have any memories, he didn't even have words. He was a being dislodged from everything and finding himself thanklessly, mercilessly alive.

Slowly I crept back into my flat, toward the ringing screams of my father. I glanced back, knowing better but unable to control myself, and my mother was gone, back around the corner of our kitchen in Istanbul—returning perhaps to my father now arriving through the front door. After all, if she was in there, was another he there with her? The father who loves me because he remembers me, because he knows me, because he knows everything again? Outside my bedroom, I found him crawling on the floor, crying out in anger.

Had I been back to my own flat? I must have. I remembered moments when, standing in a trance in front of the oven, the timer would ding, but what had I been cooking? The pill bottle that was running low was suddenly full again, though I couldn't recall refilling the prescription. It occurred to me that the prison was fizzling my own memory, corroding it to match my father's, so that

I couldn't say for sure the last time I saw him. It must've been today, this morning, but as soon as I thought back to morning, the image of its sunrise paled, dissolved, and became instead every sunrise of my life. From the cell, life outside prison appeared like a dream, waterlogged, surreal. We were running so low on money that I had been skipping meals and, without me telling him, my father too had begun skipping meals. It was horrible counting out the pennies for individual packets of oatmeal. When I bent down to lift him from his chair, my father was terribly light.

April had snuck up on me. The countryside around Baronissi had thawed and the wide days of spring stretched their arms and yawned, and we, like hibernating bears lumbering down from the Apennines, were lean and famished. On one of my trips to the pharmacy I was struck by the trees in the parks putting on their buds in white, pink, red, purple; little balloons up and down the twigs, even growing as they sometimes do in clumps on the trunks and thick branches, like small tumors, little pads of cancer so brightly arrayed. I plucked a handful, stuffing them into my pockets to take home to my father. It was his last spring, surely—limpid skies, uninspired weather, porcelain, and yet I could not shake the sense that it was the first spring of my life. In my pocket, I squeezed the buds between my fingers, their softness surprising, like I had never pinched a flower before. Hurrying home (had I collected the pills?), I went to my father and presented him with my harvest. I pressed it into his hand, crushed the buds and spread their pieces across his palm, staining its wrinkles with a soft mist of pollen. I pressed his last spring into his hand and into my own and I brought it up to our faces, the green, fresh odor. It tasted as it smelled, and my tongue was gritty from pollen. He stared unmoved, uncomprehending at the mess of petals.

I took the remaining buds with me into the cell, to share this velvety paste with the women of the prison. It was their first spring too, I knew, and I would paint the fine hairs of their arms with it.

The most thoroughly, and indeed expertly, practiced activity in the prison was the collaborative building of rumors. The women humbly brought their fancies and insidious imaginations together during mealtimes, or the long, unsupervised afternoons in their cells, but especially during the recreation period, in the small yard now glutted in sunlight. They'd construct such tall tales about the guards, making them characters in their own elaborate soap operas, or embellish on the exploits of their families back home, or even speculate on famous actors and singers who had, failing rehab, found themselves imprisoned as well and were now slinking down these very halls. And of course, they gossiped about the prison itself, the center and limit of our very small universe.

"They're definitely expanding it. I've heard the construction crews when we're out in the yard."

"That's not new," I said. "They've been building it the whole time." The supervisor had told me as much, but I didn't know if it was true.

I hadn't seen Müge since the earthquake. Did she miss me? Did she wonder what might've happened to me? Self-pity convinced me she hadn't even noticed. Another girl who had been standing nearby sat down next to me on the concrete and leaned in with an air of secrecy. "They are always expanding prisons. I'm at the end of my row. I wake up yesterday and there's a cell on my left with a girl in it. Where did that come from?"

"You just never looked beyond your own feet," said another.

"They've got the election coming up. They need more rooms in this hotel," an old woman with a bit of a hunch said. "Any time there is an election, you can bet the prisons are getting new wings."

They often discussed the election, mentioned a sense of impending victory. Whose victory exactly they didn't say, but it was obvious they meant a victory for themselves, a victory for those creatures you find when turning over rocks on the riverbank. The younger ones spoke with such conviction, such righteous anger about the changes to come, but the older ones did not disparage or discourage them, instead speaking sweetly of impossibilities like a general pardon, as was fashionable in the fifties, sixties, and seventies. I swallowed up as much of their hope as I could stand—the poorest commodity—before returning to my flat across the sea.

Every election or referendum since we left Turkey, I had invested an incautious amount of hope in the idea that Erdoğan would fall and we could return to Istanbul. The end of Erdoğan's regime would be the end of exile, the end of my distance from relatives, the end of the impossible homesickness. I would arise rejuvenated. I would visit my cousins and my aunts and my uncle, and they would all be just as before. Those seven years now heavy as the midday sun would fall away, collapsing us into each other, collapsing me into all the missed moments. I could already taste the lamb kofte from my favorite little kebab shop, the sticky lokma I would buy from the old confectioner's in Bebek. The rip of engines would jump down alleys, their diesel wakes lingering in the nose. Cats would come out onto the balconies and mew welcomes until the fog and the rain came in sliding panes over the city, and little slugs would crawl out onto the apartment steps each night to sing their sluggy songs.

The opposition was polling ahead of Erdoğan. The country was unified in its grievances against the regime. I looked at plane tickets. I told my aunts I missed them.

I had hoped my aunts would call on election day. Or my husband. Or Lucia, or the pharmacist, or the neighbors, or the contractor, or anyone. I must have looked very silly, pacing from the kitchen to my bedroom, from bedroom to front door, front door to my father's room that evening, checking the news feed on my laptop, turning on and off the lights for something to do, sighing, searching the corners and ceilings and behind the couch cushions and under the rugs like I would find in them my fate.

Where was my husband now? Watching the election updates in a café? What café, at this hour, in this country, would be running updates on the Turkish election? Or was he at a library, on a computer, scrolling, scrolling? Why hadn't he called me?

I'm sure we could go back, I would tell him.

In time, yes. In time.

Right now, right away, there's not a moment to spare! The coffers are emptied and the cobwebs of hunger are spun so thick in the corners of my stomach!

But, Dilara, it can't be so immediate. There is so much to change. My father would have agreed with him. Real change was a matter of long and continual effort, not some cheap catharsis that dispels—in an instant, at the stroke of midnight—decades of injustice.

Why not? We have done our part! We have said our will, voiced our voice, snapped our fingers, disbanded these jealous autocrats and sycophants, and remade the world to match its people. My god, when did I get so sentimental? But why not—lives are at stake! My life, my life is at stake, mine mine mine. Time has run out, the pantry pillaged, the pill bottles tipped and hollow. Return us to our country! Now, now!

In time, yes. In time.

Tomorrow, tonight, this minute! Strip away this life, this Italian dream, this festooned exile!

In time, yes. In time.

I haven't got it. I haven't got any time. I haven't—

In time, yes. In time.

Hear me! I—

In time, yes. In time.

I am crushed, absolutely crushed—

In time—
Yes, in time.

This evening, I saw the horrible news: the election was too close to call. The candidates would face each other in a runoff in two weeks. I feared the opposition had run out of steam, but even if they managed to snatch a victory— even if Kemal Kılıçdaroğlu turned out to be more than a Band-Aid over an amputation—there would be no return. The political firebrand that was one cousin (who, last I saw him, was quoting de Beauvoir and Sartre) had grown up into a cautious doctor of philosophy, married now and quiet, scared of the regime. His mother, the dancing, cursing, haggling aunt, was now an arthritic septuagenarian, living with her sister whose spine was being swallowed by osteoporosis. The two of them stayed home most nights in their shared flat, in bed early. Another cousin, the son of my industrialist uncle, had given up regattas and the hedonist's life for a position in his father's company, which was, like all companies in Turkey, faltering under the tremendous burden of an economy in a tailspin. I longed to see my family, full to the brim with love for them, but we were now seven-year strangers. Would I even recognize them?

It felt like the city itself had conspired against me to make itself unknown and unrecognizable. The protesters at Gezi Park had been trying to stop Erdoğan from converting one of the few remaining green spaces into a neo-Ottoman arcade and they had lost, one of many construction programs initiated under the regime for the simulacrum of progress and development. Under Erdoğan, Istanbul and the rest of the country had seen a construction craze, with bridges, tunnels, plazas, complexes, malls, and roads going up, seemingly overnight, the contracts handed to inexperienced and incompetent builders who ignored building codes and concealed safety violations unpunished, exacerbating the natural disasters when they struck, and causing constant calamity at Soma and other mines and industrial centers across the country. An enormous new airport welcomed millions of visitors to Istanbul every year. Yavuz Sultan Selim Bridge cut across the northern end of the strait, and work had begun on the Istanbul Canal, west of the Bosporus, ignoring experts' warnings that the project would be an environmental and geological disaster. The Ayasofya had been converted back into a mosque, Kız Kulesi dismantled and rebuilt. Galata Tower was "renovated" with jackhammers. Ancient mosaics were restored into laughable deformities of their previous selves. Meanwhile sea snot had invaded the Aegean and killed off dozens of species in the Marmara— soon fresh-caught fish would be a thing of the past in Istanbul's restaurants. All across the country, lakes were drying up and dams were flooding millennia-old villages and historic sites. And of course the very names of things in Turkey changed constantly. They had renamed the Bosporus Bridge to 15 July Martyrs Bridge shortly after the failed coup. Kızılay Square became 15 July Kızılay Democracy Square. The Grand Istanbul Bus Station became

Istanbul 15 July Democracy Bus Station. Before that, they changed the taxonomical names of three animals to remove references to Armenia and Kurdistan. Since the Republic, they've changed the names of thousands of cities, towns, and villages. The streets changed names every generation or so, and in the east, sometimes a village would get all new Turkish road signs over the Kurdish ones. The country had even forced a change of its own name, a PR stunt as wars erupted on its borders, financial meltdowns tanked the economy, and corruption scandal after corruption scandal splashed the headlines. Turkey's names were changed and changing—a state-sanctioned act of collective memory to further entrench the regime in the foundations of the country so that Erdoğan's legacy would be subsuming the state entirely into his person. They think it means something when the government changes the name, they think it grants them authority-through-act, as if their own names won't one day settle along the silt of all the other names. Some days I believed places are endless and immortal, unhampered by these paper-anchor names, and other days I truly feared that the name is the sum total of a thing, the cold new word prizing it away from itself moment by moment. Beyoğlu was Pera and they are entirely different cities. Istanbul was Konstantiniyye, was Constantinople, was Alma Roma, was Augusta Antonina, was Byzantion, was Lygos—the impossibility of continuity. A place was the sum of its names.

The Istanbul I had dreamed of returning to was not just a fabrication of memory but something clouded completely by naivete. I had deluded myself for seven years that ousting Erdoğan, watching him lose, would somehow give me back everything I had missed. It would give me back my grandparents' funerals, my cousins' weddings, the births of their children. Turkey, this country that had obsessed my dreams and left me hollowed out at the foot of its immense mesmerism, was only a place of the past. As with childhood's magic frontiers, there was no way to travel back once you had left.

I had grown careless. I must have. Someone, or two, or more women had seen a soda bottle on my table, or my laundry basket at the end of the cot, or one of my succulents, or my electric kettle with its extension cable coming out from the doorway behind the partition like an absurd umbilical cord. What did it matter; they found out about the doorway through which I could, at any moment I wished, walk out of this cage to a flat in Italy.

The women confronted me that evening, after the guards left and doused the lights. At once, their voices rang out from each cell, betrayed, furious. "Who are you," they demanded of me, "who are you and what are you doing here as a cruel imposter?" Up and down the long hallway the women's voices rose up, on the verge of tears with rage, and I could hear them rattle their hearts against the bars of their cells.

"What are you talking about?" I asked as innocently as I could manage.

"Don't lie, don't lie, it's no use anyway," they said. "There's a door in your cell, a door that leaves the prison."

"How absurd."

"Don't lie, don't lie, it's no use anyway," they said. "There's a door in your cell."

"Says who?"

"I do," said Müge, her voice wavering. "I say." It stung like the heat from a slap.

"We will rouse the guards. We'll tell them everything," the women said, "unless you take us with you."

Suddenly the whole prison was very quiet to me. Everyone carried on shouting as much as ever, but their voices reached me from a long way off.

"Save us, save us," they said.

"I cannot save you; the guards won't open the cells."

"Save us, save us," they said.

"I cannot save you; I am only one woman."

"Save us, save us," they said.

"And where would you go, thrown against the rocky shore of Italy? I can hardly stand it here myself!"

"Save us!" they cried.

I could not speak; there wasn't space for it. There was no explanation I could submit to dissuade them. It seemed it would go on forever, this terrible and invisible procession of agony. But really, who was the betrayer and who betrayed? In the end, what could I say but that I would save them?

I told them we would need a plan. We would need time to prepare. I asked them not to get impatient because I would need to take out a loan, and rent tools, and maybe hire an Italian to help, but we could start cutting the bars and chiseling the walls very soon, very soon, just please keep quiet about all this until then.

My husband called me from a pay phone outside Milan. "It's very difficult to find a pay phone here," is how he said hello. He asked me if I was healthy and remembering to eat something better than the meals I made for Dad. I reminded him I didn't want him to call me anymore, but I couldn't bring myself to hang up.

"I'm worried sick about you," he said.

"You always say that," I said. "Your stomach must be perpetually tied into a knot."

"You should've left with me."

"Aren't you bored of this?" I asked him. He was not being inventive at all, which at that moment I wanted more than anything in the world. I wanted him to say something surprising, something a poet might tell a lover, although in my limited experience poets were the worst people to ask for something clever off the cuff. Writers become writers because there is no off-the-cuff for them.

"Dilara, are you listening to me? I'm worried sick!"

"No. You don't get to say that. You are not sick. You are not worried." I demanded he say something, anything else. I demanded he get his money's worth out of that pay phone. I demanded it the way I sometimes imagine I might demand from God, should I ever make His acquaintance, an explanation for this His creation.

"I'm coming to get you."

"From a pay phone outside Milan?"

"I am buying a train ticket. I am coming to get you."

This was uncharted territory. Coming back to the flat with a prison in it? "Well, I'm not going," I said, the words jumping out of me.

"Pack your bags." The way he said it, the confidence of the command, half tricked me that he would come down from Milan after all, that he had already loaded the phone booth onto a train now departing for Salerno.

Playful in my contrarianism, my voice becoming almost a song: "No, no, I'm not going."

"You don't have a choice," he said.

Tickled by this threat of kidnap that was fast becoming a game for me, I egged him on, practically rocking in my seat as I told him that I would not go willingly, I would need to be dragged out of here kicking and screaming, I would need to be rescued. I laughed and laughed, thinking of him showing up, lifting me into a taxi, the two of us fleeing. My husband would come down from Milan and his presence would become a solution instead of a problem, yes, there was time for it yet, there was time for my life to be righted.

"You should've left with me," my husband said—the moment passed, a joke stretched so thin as to become gossamer and then nothing.

I closed my eyes. "Dad isn't moving anymore."

"Are you . . . I mean . . . I'm just so worried—"

"Shut up. Shut up. Shut up. I mean it, shut up. I can't take it. Shut up. Shut up," but I couldn't hang up.

My husband said, as if falling into the sky: "Wouldn't

it be nice if you could get away to where your father can't hurt you anymore?"

It sounded like he was inviting me to my own funeral. Pain is life, after all. Painlessness is death, and I have my very own father as evidence.

He used to take things in his gaze. Actively and intensely, he held on to them, as if he were laboring to understand them, imbue them with meaning, so that when he picked up the honey jar again, he would know not to bounce it like a tennis ball. It was like hunger. Watching him was like watching a winter-famished wolf greedily eat every morsel of the forest—jubilant and proud and covetous. But even this had faded. His handsome eyes had fled and now stuck into his face were these mute and insensitive marbles, blind eyes pinned to a greatly distanced point, and he was a husk, an old man who had misplaced himself.

I thought my father was better off losing his mind, saved from the pain of remembering. Now he is free from the country that calls him a traitor, with all its miserable squabbles. Now his wife is no longer dead, she hardly even existed in the first place, soon she will be gone entirely. Looking out the window, he won't see his old neighborhood anymore. He won't see the hills of Ortaköy from our living room. And he won't see Italy either.

I had envied him this, but I did not, in truth, desire the same fate, even if Turkey seemed to desire it out from under me, the way it conspired to change. But I had not been faithful to it, so why shouldn't it change and leave me behind? "While my back is turned you become someone else!" I accuse it, and it replies, "To say *while your back is turned* implies that you will ever turn around again."

I don't want to miss my country anymore. I want a self-renovation of the soul. I want an erasure like the controlled burns on the steppes, the immolations that remove the thistles and noxious weeds, the stover and dry grasses. I want to take up a driptorch and set fire to my insides until everything that was gold is turned to charcoal—an act of preservation. My charred heart will not rot or decay. Could I flee? How could I abandon my father? Though isn't it true that he has already left me behind?

Two or three years ago, we took a short holiday with Lucia and Giovanni. They had a place in the Aosta Valley, a surprisingly cramped condo compared to the opulent chalet I had expected, and they had invited us to join them skiing. They gave us odds and ends of borrowed gear, hand-me-downs, and some items produced by generous neighbors who were there mostly for views rather than sport. We looked like a diagram of changing ski apparatus over the decades.

My husband skied very well, lazily well almost, as if he'd skied every winter. "I grew up doing it," he admitted. "Though it's been almost fifteen years." I hadn't known this about him. He was so obviously at ease on the slope, the rhythmic and slicing shush of his skis across the snow was hypnotic to watch, and the casualness of his effort inspired the sense that I too could be a great skier. The opposite was true. I hadn't clicked the second boot in before I fell and tangled my poles so badly with my skis that I had to be hauled up by Giovanni, my husband, and a passing stranger. Within the hour, my husband had begun to abandon me to my crashes (after I assured him multiple times that I would be fine) in order to go on a quick run with Gian before riding the lift to the top and catching me back up. I had never gotten far in the interim, and he laughed so gleefully that I couldn't possibly be upset with him.

Lucia didn't ski. "It leaves such bright purple bruises all over my shins. I look like a delinquent footballer." So my husband was stuck vacillating between coddling me down the greens and following Giovanni through increasingly difficult runs. I felt bad for holding him up, depriving him of picking up right where he'd left this sport off as a young man in the mountains just south of Ankara. Still, he seemed content to spend most of his time slightly above me, shouting helpful suggestions about leaning and turning until I lost balance or caught the back of my ski and wiped out in a cloud of powder. He would be beside me in a flash, planting his skis firmly in the snow and pulling me back onto my feet before setting me off with the most encouraging little push. Normally I would've called this kind of advice patronizing, but it was always so good-natured and genuine, and something in me stifled my natural inclinations to sulking whenever I wasn't immediately good at a task. The sun was out—the snow a blinding sheet under a pine-fringed sky. I remember thanking Giovanni as we rode back up the lift. "He's never been happier," I said of my husband.

"You're both in good spirits," he smiled, and I realized I'd been repeating over and over how thrilling it was to ski, how sore my abdomen was from full-bellied laughter at each of my many falls.

On the last run of the day, I had managed to stay upright nearly the entire course before, at the end, it dropped into a steeper incline. I went back and forth as my husband coached me from behind, taking great pride in my improvement in such a short amount of time. Then, the last turn back across the slope, I caught a groove and went tumbling, head over heels multiple times down to the bottom. My husband was once again there in a moment, shouting, asking if I was hurt. In his haste and boisterousness, he couldn't hear me chuckling between exhausted groans. When he shushed right alongside me, I tripped him with my pole and brought him down, and I pounced on him. I kissed him and kissed him, the skis trapping my legs rather awkwardly, until a passing skier asked if we needed help up.

"You're happy," I said to my husband.

"Yes." He struggled out from under me and lay back on the slope under the sun-bleached sky. "Are you happy?"

"Italy is like a stepfather country," I said. I'm not sure why. The thought struck me only the moment I said it, but it seemed like he might understand.

"No," he said. "There is a home and there is a homeland, and they aren't always the same."

Lucia had a thick potato soup waiting for us, then plenty of hot drinks and schnapps. We talked and joked into the early evening when we three skiers, drained from the slopes and the constant laughter during dinner, practically fell asleep in our seats over an easy game of cards. I hadn't, until nearly the end of the drive home, thought once of my father.

In no time, I had the living room cleared of anything that might trip my father. On the kitchen counter was a basket of potatoes, some of them already spurting their warty new sprouts through the braids. I hoped they might clone into a river of potatoes running down the faces of my cabinets. The fridge was full of three or four dozen small, airtight containers with cured meats and smoked cheeses in them. The pantry was nothing but sleeves of crackers. I wrote on a hundred, maybe two hundred sticky notes the phrase "food in the refrigerator." Some were just the word REFRIGERATOR in bold capitals. I stuck them all throughout the house, on cupboard handles, faucets, at the window locks, in sock drawers, on clothes hangers, in teacups, by the water kettle, on the faces of books and any other flat surface, and over the peephole at the front door. I left the door unlocked. Finally, I placed one on the arm of my father's recliner. It was just a drawing, crudely, of our fridge.

"Can you read it?"

"Something, eh?" He scratched a weeping sore in the fold of his nostril.

"Dad," I said, taking his fingers softly from his face, holding his hand in mine, pressing it into first one of my palms then the other, a sticky spill of drying blood stamped onto my skin. "Dad."

"Who?"

"You," I said, trying to kiss the back of his fingers, but something like choking stopped me.

"Something," he said over and over. Looking past me, over my shoulder to the window, he whispered at last: "Who?"

"Dad."

He withdrew his hand and slowly uncurled away from me, back into his chair, his face wincing as if the room was hurtling away from him. It was just noon and all the shadows had come undone—the opposite of blindness.

I piled a few provisions by the door, small things you might take on a hike, if you weren't the sort of person who normally hiked: a bag of chocolates, a bottle of soda water, a sleeve of crackers, a few blocks of white cheese, instant coffee. Next to these I folded up a bundle of clothes and my toiletries and some good books. Then I fetched the huge bucket I had bought from the hardware shop and started to mix the mortar. I chucked my things into the cell and started stacking the bricks, spreading mortar carefully between them. From inside the prison, I built a wall sealing me off from my bedroom, sealing me in the cell, in Silivri, in Turkey. Maybe they will let me out in a few years. Maybe, if the regime is ousted, there'll be a general pardon like there used to be.

I'd slathered all the mortar, so I mixed up some more and started a second wall of bricks covering the first. As I went, I could feel the breeze come off the Bosporus and the sun climb high overhead, where it stayed perched as I worked, but it was not unpleasant—in fact, the boughs of a few Judas trees came to cover me and fill me with the sweet scent of their new leaves. When I reached for another brick, I saw that the floor around me was a cobblestone esplanade over the Bosporus, where jellyfish and little darting creatures bobbed about the surface. Behind me now was the gleaming Ortaköy Mosque, with the high, sweeping line of the bridge beyond it. Before me were the walled gardens and apartments of a palace, and deeper into the mist came the familiar rolling hills of the city, flat as paper on my eyes. I could hear the fishmongers shout out their prices, and I watched the caïques and tankers lolling across the sea. As I pressed the last brick into place, I could taste the brine and the flower buds and the spices from the bazaar. I could hear the gulls and the motorway. I saw fishermen fix their nets in the sun and lovers tear their hair out at the scope of their affections. All of it was crammed, crammed into the cell. All of the city was in there with me—all of the country. It swirled in a great and terrible form, as if everything I had ever loved and feared had been scooped out of me and thrown into a kaleidoscope. My body was in a cell in Silivri Prison, and it would now never leave it.

ACKNOWLEDGMENTS

I would like to thank my agent, Martha Wydysh, and my editors, Milo Walls and Hermione Thompson, all of them insightful, dedicated, and, importantly, the most generous and caring readers.

Thanks also to *The Atlantic* and the very kind Oliver Munday for publishing the short story out of which this novel grew.

And lastly, a deep if insufficient thank-you to my partner, Ashton, whose warmth, support, and affection have made ours a lopsided love I could never balance.

A Note About the Author

Kenan Orhan's debut collection, *I Am My Country and Other Stories*, was a finalist for the PEN/Robert W. Bingham Prize and was long-listed for the Story Prize. His fiction has appeared in *The Atlantic, The Paris Review, The Common, Massachusetts Review,* and other publications and has been anthologized in *The O. Henry Prize Stories* and *The Best American Short Stories. The Renovation* is his first novel.